In the Shade of the Terebinth

In the Shade of the Terebinth

TALES OF A NIGHT JOURNEY

Gabriel Meyer

Forest of Peace
Publishing

Suppliers for the Spiritual Pilgrim

In the Shade of the Terebinth

Library of Congress Cataloging-in-Publication Data
Meyer, Gabriel, 1947-
    In the shade of the terebinth: tales of a night journey / Gabriel Meyer.
        p.   cm.
    ISBN: 0-939516-23-3
    1. Bible. N.T.—History of Biblical events—Fiction.   I. Title.
    PS3563.E873I5   1994
    813' .54—dc20   94-583
                                                                 CIP

published by
Forest of Peace Publishing, Inc.
PO Box 269
Leavenworth, KS 66048-0269 USA

printed by
Jostens, Inc.

illustrated by
Michael Schrauzer

first printing: March 1994

For Fran Maier,

without whose steadfast encouragement and assistance

this book would still be

in the drawer

The *terebinth* of the title is the *pistacia atlantica*, the Atlantic terebinth, one of four species of the ancient tree native to Israel. Terebinths today are to be found principally in the Negev, Lower Galilee and the Dan Valley where they can attain both great size and age.

Because of the similarity of the tree's biblical name (*elah*) with the word for oak (*elon*), the terebinth has often been rendered "oak" in English bibles. As the names suggest, both trees were deified by the ancients (*el*, "god"). And like the oak, terebinth stands were frequently honored as places of worship and as burial sites for esteemed dead. Even today, Bedouin have been known to bury their dead beneath the terebinth.

CONTENTS

Like a terebinth,
Wisdom spreads out her branches,
and her branches
are glorious and graceful.

Sirach 24:16

I

The thing had literally dropped into his hand like an acorn.

He'd had to blink at it for several moments in the noonday glare—when the limestone blinds—before he could tell just what had fallen into his upturned palm. A stone tossed down from the heaven of high courtyard windows to annoy him? A dying air-borne insect determined to flutter to the last in his hand's shallow grave?

The boy still remembered the day when his cousin called him to witness the discovery of a silkworm cocoon, found on the stone stairs while sweeping. The stain-brown fibers had been pulled apart to reveal the butterfly, twitching in death.

To harm such creatures, the old women scolded them, was very bad luck indeed. And Issa, for one, believed them. To this day, the boy imagined, on occasion, that he could feel butterflies tremble against his eyelids in the last moments before sleep.

But it was not the carcass of an insect which he fingered under the gaze of the yellow-dust Jerusalem sky. It was a small black ring.

The happiness of sudden adventure nearly took the poor boy's breath away.

Who knows whose this might be, he thought, or how it came to fall into my hand? Stolen perhaps from the tables of the rich by a clever hawk? (Such things had been known to happen.) Thrown from a nearby roof by an angry spouse? Something jostled loose from the heart of the oak by children? A ring fashioned by mystics for a secret bride?

(Unlike the other children, this one paid attention to the songs sung by the women around the laundry tubs.)

The idea suddenly crossed his mind that Henry might have had something to do with it. Henry: the brass man, huddled in his musty little room muttering to himself— Henry: surrounded by metal trinkets, crusts of stale uneaten bread and the half-finished beaten-brass models of the city's monuments he hammered out for tourists.

No, Issa thought, it's too early in the day. Poor Henry won't crawl out of the covers of his brandybottle dreams for hours yet. In any case, the brass man had never been known to part with a piece of jewelry like that—jewelry that could be sold.

Issa opened and closed his fingers hard upon the object— the metal strangely hot to the touch. There it was, gazing out of the cocoon of his hand like a newborn insect: the thin black ring with the two large bezels—their surfaces hard-edged as the backs of beetles.

It was an omen, surely. Even Issa, a mere boy, knew that much. But the immediate problem which confronted him as he stood there in the open square, alone, under the sleepy noon-time gaze of the neighbors, had precious little to do with unraveling the ring's mysteries. The first order of business, in fact, was to hide it. Issa knew that one false move on his part, the slightest hint of the body language of possession, would bring the rough hands of his playmates upon him and his adventure like locusts.

And so, without saying a word to anyone, even to his mother, Issa deposited the ring into the pocket of his old much-mended caftan and shot fast as a stone out of the hot white courtyard.

"Exactly where did you find the ring?" old Shukri inquired—the dark band poised between his fingers.

Though he'd witnessed the routine a thousand times, the sight of the blind old merchant examining an object with everything but his eyes nearly always reduced the boy to silence.

Fingers, nose, ears, teeth—all were summoned to aid in the assessment that went on behind the thick black lenses the blind man wore.

In fact, Shukri's uncanny "eye"—as the locals called it—had made him the chief assessor of goods on Christian Quarter Road, the old city's crowded paradise of merchants. Silver-smith, antique dealer, junkman, raconteur, magistrate: that was Shukri. On any given day, dozens of people—scholars, con men, bedouin, curators, thieves—would find their way here, placing their would-be treasures on the old man's dusty counter. A local wit had long ago dubbed the routine "the weighing of souls."

For Issa, of course, the bond with the "Wonder of Christian Quarter Road" was more elemental: a boy whose own father was a shadow, barely a name, had found care, and more, in the workshop of the childless old man.

Shukri was taking his time about the ring, the boy observed happily. This was to be expected. Only the old Syrian could be trusted to take the time to know a thing's true value.

While he awaited the craftsman's verdict, the boy let his eyes wander about the narrow shop's jumble of discarded, discovered merchandise. For him, it was a never-ending source of mystery—though, as a daily visitor—and Shukri's helper—he knew the whereabouts of practically everything. As his eyes surveyed Shukri's familiar, yet fantastic, world of topsy-turvy jars and chests and cupboards, it suddenly occurred to the boy that what he'd really come to the old man for was something more than an appraisal. He hadn't sped here like the wind simply in order to find a safe haven for a poor boy's treasure. He'd come to Shukri, the man he most trusted in the world, to find out what the ring meant.

Issa found himself whispering a prayer to old St. Parakletos the Fatherless whose image hung, flanked by a votive light, in the deep recesses of the shop.

"O Mirror of Damascus...," Issa cantillated the words as he'd heard Shukri do.

Parakletos—the name was Greek for "consolation"—was a Syrian holy man who'd been orphaned as a child. Like Shukri, he'd ended up not in Damascus—where he was still honored as the patron of abandoned children—but, for reasons unknown, in Jerusalem.

The boy had listened once to Shukri explain to a customer the merchant's own reasons for coming to the Holy City some years ago from the great Syrian capital.

"Does it seem strange to you that a silversmith would leave the bazaars of Damascus for a jeweler's stall in Jerusalem?" he had remarked. "Well," he'd laughed, "let's just say one can be too well known in a place like Damascus.

"In any case, you can't be unaware that Jerusalem's holy ones—the Apostles themselves—fled to Syria when the Romans besieged the Holy City in the time of the Emperor Titus, or that the bones of John the Baptist sleep in Damascus, or that we Syrians still have the language of Jesus on our tongues."

At the time Issa had not understood much of what the old man was saying, but, for some reason, the words remained in his mind, especially the ones Shukri had used to close the conversation: "There are many mysterious connections between Damascus and Jerusalem—of that I can assure you."

Shukri rarely spoke of such things—his past—and never to

Issa. A few silent rebuffs to a casual question or two had been enough to teach the boy not to ask.

"Well, Baba," Issa said at last, unable to contain his curiosity about the ring any longer. "Tell me what you think!"

Turning, he found the merchant, much to his surprise, standing perfectly still, as if transfixed—frozen—by memory. Issa had never seen the old man like this before.

"Baba!" Issa cried, in the diminutive reserved for fathers. "What is it? Are you ill?"

Shukri didn't speak at first, contenting himself with a long sigh. Finally, his sightless gaze still lowered on the object in his hand, the Syrian said once more: "Where did you find this, son? Did...someone give it to you?"

"Oh, no. I really found it. Or the ring found me, I should say."

Shukri was smiling now, to Issa's relief. "And how does a ring find a boy?" Shukri said.

"It fell out of the sky," said Issa, gesturing wildly. "Well," he added with a grin, "I think it really fell from the tree, from the oak in the courtyard. You know, the old one."

Shukri turned slowly to light the Bunsen burner for tea. Issa offered his help, but he knew beforehand that the old man would insist on tending to it himself.

"Pomegranates, apples, olives, almonds—all these I've found in trees. Never rings," Shukri continued, skeptically.

"Shall I tell you what I think?" Issa said excitedly.

"Please." The old Syrian asked Issa to pour a little of the concentrated tea he'd boiled that dawn into two small glasses.

"Well, you know better than I that the old oak is no ordinary tree."

Indeed, everyone knew that. The courtyard over which the venerable oak presided, where Issa lived with his mother

Myrna, was a neighborhood weli, a holy place, the forgotten tomb of some long-forgotten sheikh—so well-forgotten, in fact, that locals called the place "Courtyard of the No-Name Saint." There were hundreds of such shrines scattered about the city, nearly every street or alley had one.

But Issa's otherwise anonymous holy tree had at least one distinction. It had over the years become a modest place of pilgrimage for poor women deserted by their husbands. There, by the grave of Saint "No-Name," they wept their copious tears, vastly enriching, it must be added, the courtyard's store of gossip in the process.

"*Ya, ya, ya, y'abba,*" the women would cry, often carting along their fatherless children to stimulate the saint's interest.

"Cover your daughter with the wings of a good name," their song ran, "to the feet of her humiliations"—that last a word upon which the petitioners invariably lingered.

"Yes, well?" Shukri was flavoring the tea with twigs of dried sage called *miramiyeh*, after the Blessed Virgin Mary.

"But don't you see?" cried Issa. "People are always hanging things on the oak—to make the saint take notice. Rags, keys, ribbons, photos, medals, anything...why not a ring?"

Even now the boy could visualize the magic tree spreading its noisy ragtag wings of mercy over all his world like a Providence.

The old merchant set the two glasses of steaming tea on the counter. Issa lifted his gingerly with thumb and forefinger to avoid the heat of the glass. Only his mother made tea better than old Shukri, he said to himself as he sipped the syrup-sweet drink.

"Maybe it was tied on something. A breeze might have blown it down."

"Take some more *miramiyeh* in your tea, Issa," Shukri

14

said. "To keep you from summer colds."

Issa, who knew the old man as well as he knew anyone, could clearly see from Shukri's manner that the merchant was thinking hard about something. It was evident to the boy in the way the old man stirred his tea—slowly, absently. How often he had watched the old man behave like this as he calculated the value of an antique lamp or a ceramic jar.

"It's over tea that he decides your fate," one of the wily merchant's confreres told a buyer once.

"The ring did not fall from the tree, Issa. Not like you think." The voice, though Shukri's, seemed to come from a long distance. "It was placed there."

Because Shukri was blind, his demeanor always had something of an inscrutable air about it. That was what made him such a formidable haggler. But Issa, in all the years he'd known the old merchant, had never seen such a mask descend over his features. As though invisible wounds had opened.

"But how? By whom?"

But the old man had turned his face away.

Just then Henry the brass-man peered into the shop looking for Shukri. His gangly frame was silhouetted against the streetworld's veils of light and dust.

The brass man was one of Shukri's regular afternoon visitors. On a normal day, heaving his sack of clanking metal onto the old man's counter, he'd inquire after sales of his handiwork and stay for tea. Today, however, was not a normal day—not even for Henry. The brass man's dark unshaven face wore a wary look.

As for Shukri, he was clearly in no mood to humor him. The boy noticed that he forgot even to offer him tea.

Instead, the merchant, without so much as a greeting, asked Henry to make himself useful for once and write a message for him: a message, he said, for Issa's mother.

"You wouldn't mind staying with old Shukri tonight, would you?" the old man said to Issa before he muttered something in Henry's ear.

Mind? The boy turned over the thought. Staying with Shukri: a full stomach and glasses of tea and stories when the old man's heart was glad. Staying with Shukri: a deep sleep under the warm surface of thick wool blankets, a respite from cold stone floors and the cacophony of the neighbors' bitter curses.

Not that he and his mother lived in dire poverty any longer. For several years now, a mysterious but providential hand always seemed to bless them when they hovered on the brink of want.

Issa laughed: the day's second promise of adventure. (And all because of a tree and its secrets!)

His dictation done, Henry was hustled out of the shop. But not before he'd whispered a hoarse gold-toothed complaint to his next-door neighbor.

"Heard you found something," the lean young man said.

Issa's eyes grew wide.

"Well, you should've shown it to me first. Now," he warned, wagging his nicotine-stained finger at the boy, "there'll be talk."

"What are you doing there?" Shukri growled, advancing on the man from behind the counter with his cane. "Leave the boy alone," he shouted, shoving the brass man out into the street. Issa heard Henry mumble something as he ambled off— something about "that woman."

"I'm warning you...," the old merchant barked as the brass man sped off around the corner.

Issa, suddenly fearful of what lay in store for him at home, among the denizens of "No-Name" courtyard, did something he'd not done for a long time. He pressed his head into the old man's apron.

Everyone will know now, Issa said to himself. Everyone will say that Issa is a thief. He could already hear the songs the boys would make up to mock him. And the women? To him, they will say nothing. But they will make *her* life miserable. They will say that Issa's mother is to blame.

The boy glanced up at the old man. He expected to see the flex of hard neck muscles, the working of the lower jaw— tokens of his row with the brass man. Instead, a strange peace reigned over the familiar features. Even the marks of age seemed to have been smoothed from his face. As Issa watched him—the waning daylight reflected in the twin black mirrors which veiled him—the old man looked like one who, after many hesitations, has decided at last on a course of action.

"Come, let's take a look at your prize," he said finally, summoning Issa to a counter stool.

There were long minutes of fiddling to get the loupe in place before the old man could let Issa get a look at the ring. But, examine as he might, the more the boy explored the surface of the treasure, the less he understood about it:

> The twin black beetles' humps,
> smooth to the touch as Dead Sea pebbles,
> the stone face grained with white tattoos
> like a Berber's.
> Issa counted them:
> thirteen, maybe fourteen fine-lined characters
> only faintly visible without a glass,
> hanging in the branches of a sprawling tree—
> or was it some sort of figure?
> He couldn't exactly tell.

Only the filigree vines encircling the band seemed familiar. Damascus work. Issa had watched Shukri spin out silver filigree before, filigree like this, filigree fine as lace. Only, Issa thought, the workmanship here is even better than the old man's, even more delicate, and his is the best in Jerusalem.

"I knew it," the boy said finally.

"What do you know?" the old man whispered, placing his hand on the boy's shoulder.

"That I'd never seen anything like this before, not ever, not on anyone. Not even on rich people or on the fingers of the bishop. Maybe," the boy said breathlessly, "there's not another ring like this in the whole world."

Shukri placed the ring inside the folds of his polishing rag and rubbed it gently between his fingers. When Issa pulled apart the oily cloth, the ring had been transformed into a creature of fire.

"It's called a scarab ring, Issa," the craftsman explained. "Scarab: because the stone is shaped like a beetle's back. It's very, very rare."

Issa watched as Shukri eased the ring onto his own finger.

"May I?"

The boy assented. It was a perfect fit.

"You're right," the old man said. "There's not another ring like this in the whole world. Only...."

Issa looked up.

"...It's not just a ring."

For the very first time, the word "secret" blew across the landscape of Issa's mind.

"It's a map," said Shukri.

Shukri pulled out several rolled sheets of paper from the dark musty cupboard where he kept his "special things." One of these rolls was bound with a ribbon.

The merchant fingered the ribbon to be sure he had the right roll before smoothing the tracing out on the counter for the boy to examine. Though faded with age, Issa could make out the outline of a spreading tree with thirteen medallions arrayed in its branches, drawn with ink in a fine hand.

On the ring itself, even under the loupe, the design had seemed a barely discernible blur of grooves. But in the drawing, Issa could make out the precise contours of the pattern inscribed on the ring: a great oak with seven rune-like designs on its right side, six on the left, all arranged in the shape of a crown.

"A tree with the crown of thirteen moons hiding in its branches. Yes, Issa?"

"Y-yes," Issa sputtered, "but...the 'moons'...there are things written on them."

"Ah," said Shukri. "I suspect you'll need some help making those out. They're not as easy to discern, even if you can see them clearly.

"There on your left is the sign of the wedding contract. And next to it the mark of the Roman cross. The key comes after that, Issa, am I right? Follow carefully with your finger and you'll be able to identify all the symbols.

"Then there's the great long-necked jar and the scroll with a seal: that's the mark of the testament," the merchant went on without a pause. "That's followed by the pieces of silver.

"On the right side of the star, we have other moons— shadows of the designs on the tree's left side—the shadow side of the great oak. The first has the mark of an olive press inside, the next a small scroll, followed by a whip, then a miniature oak tree, a jewel, a pair of dice and a small rounded perfume jar.

"That is what you see there, isn't it?" the old man concluded, his voice burnished with emotion.

There was a long silence while the boy tried to fathom what was happening to him.

"So *you* drew this!" Issa exclaimed, now thoroughly confused.

The old man shook his head.

"But who then?" the boy pressed. "And how did you...?"

"All in good time," Shukri smiled.

"But...."

"Maps are for journeys, yes?" the old man said slowly, rolling up the drawing. "You can't know what a map means unless you are prepared to follow it—first out into the great wide world and then to the places it takes us inside."

"Yes...?" said Issa, eager for more.

"Well," exclaimed the merchant, "let's go!"

"Where?" Issa cried.

But Shukri had already begun to close up shop for the night. It was a ritual Issa knew well. Each of the displays spilling prodigally into the street had its ordained place inside the cramped shop quarters: here the brace of antique chains or the basket of kerosene wicks, there the chest of old war medals or the bell-shaped jar of canes.

And then the last little procedure: as the metal shutters clattered down behind them, Shukri traced the sign of the cross with a quick sweep of his forefinger over the corrugated lucky-blue doors.

"O Virgin Mary, the Silk of Damascus," the old man muttered over his shop as he took the boy's hand and tapped his way down the now nearly-deserted arcades of Christian Quarter Road.

"Baba, where are we going?" Issa insisted.

"Can't you guess?" the old man teased. "To the first stop

20

on the journey of the ring, of course. Don't tell me you want to turn back now?" he said, laughing.

"No, no," the boy cried, already breathless.

The ring, a toy at first, had become now like a night wind sweeping Issa and all his world into a crazy dance down the dark streets of Jerusalem.

"Well then," said Shukri, settling into his best storyteller's stride, "the journey begins...

> where a great oak once grew on a hillside,
> where a girl, gathering wild pepper grasses,
> heard the breezes make a pun on her name,
> where...."

TALE OF THE
MARRIAGE CONTRACT

Menachem's hand moved with practiced poise across the surface of the smooth-buffed parchment.

> *Be my wife according to the law of Moses*
> *and of Israel....*

the black-blue letters read.

The rabbi of Nazareth put down his pen, rubbing his eyes a little. The light was bad tonight, he said to himself, rising to search for another lamp. His fingers fumbled absently in the dark bowl where wicks were kept—dried cotton-like blossoms gathered from Galilee's hillsides. A yellow glow flickered across the young man's brow as the wick, floating in a pool of golden oil, caught fire.

That was better, Menachem said, resuming. How many of these marriage contracts had he written, the rabbi wondered, since coming to the Nazareth Mountains from Jerusalem more than three years before? Hundreds surely.

There were compensations, of course. In Jerusalem, he'd had to draft official documents in Hebrew, the holy tongue, a requirement which meant doing the calligraphy in one sitting, without pause. A single misstroke of the pen, even on the very last character, and the document was spoiled. Here, thankfully, the trend was toward documents in the local *patois,* where no such rigorous pieties applied.

> *I will work for you, and maintain you*
> *in accordance with the custom of Jewish*
> *husbands....*

Menachem sing-songed the words in his mind.

As usual, he thought of the particular bridegroom whose vows he was inscribing. A smile often escaped his lips as he pondered young village men, just over the threshold of manhood, so ill-prepared for the realities of the married life they so fervently sought.

This client was different, however—in every respect. Even the contract Menachem was drafting for his marriage was unique: a second document to replace the original one inscribed for the engagement months ago, an amended contract, now replete with unusual conditions.

Yosef ben Yakov, Joseph, son of Jacob—named after the visionary son of the holy patriarch. "Best-loved of all Israel's sons," the Torah calls him. Joseph, master of dreams.

This Joseph, son of Jacob, however, had, at least until recently, been anything but a dreamer.

He was the village building contractor, what the Greeks call a *tekton*. A fine stone mason, he had a fabled eye for deposits of "sweet stone" in the hills. Skilled also in the woodcrafts of his trade, Joseph whittled the sturdy Tabor oak into yokes and wheels for the peasants.

There were other skilled craftsmen in the area, but none enjoyed Joseph's reputation for both imagination and integrity. Even Roman contractors came to him for advice. And the poor—well, they were eternally at his door, finding help with a thatch roof or a buckling wall.

It was not only his craft, however, that attracted people to the burly young man. People in Nazareth remembered Joseph best for the way he prayed. One could not easily forget the sound of that voice cantillating the Torah portion on the Sabbath.

Silence would descend on the congregation when the

builder rose to the *bimah*. In anticipation, eyes would close, senses awaken, as though fragrant spices were in the air.

Then that sound would emerge from the heart of the congregation: clear and deep as Galilee's sea, as gravely simple and graced with longing.

People said that the rare advice he offered in village meetings was "well beyond his years." Some said it had to do with his family's Davidic pedigree—a not very convincing argument since there were many families in Galilee who could claim that honor. Others—more superstitious souls—bandied it about that he was a *tsaddik*, a "just man," a hidden saint. "Perhaps there is more here than meets the eye," a few Nazareth crones had been heard to murmur meaningfully.

Joseph's more unusual habits were chiefly responsible for such talk: particularly the frequency with which he performed ritual ablutions—with him, a daily routine—perhaps a sign that he considered himself a penitent, one whose deeds are said to atone for Israel's sins.

Menachem had heard snatches of the Joseph legend even before coming to Nazareth. And, at least at first, he'd had to admit being more than a little intimidated by it.

Fortunately, for the sake of their later friendship, Nazareth's run-down synagogue desperately needed a facelift—especially now that the village had acquired the status symbol of a permanent rabbi. Nazarenes had long seethed with envy that neighboring Kefar Kana could afford to erect a two-room synagogue, complete with ritual bath, while their own even larger settlement languished with its ill-lit one-room affair, complete with drafts.

Joseph, the rabbi was told by the area's elders, was the obvious choice for the restoration.

Menachem, trained in the setting of stark Judean Judaism,

had been startled at first when the builder showed him a model of the synagogue interior which featured stone carvings of the local flora and fauna as well as faintly suspect mystical symbols like the fiery chariot of the prophet Elijah worked into the design.

For the lintel between the doors of the *Aron ha-Kodesh*, the Holy Ark, Joseph had worked out a particularly original adornment: A stately oak with thirteen stars in the shape of a crown worked into its branches. Menachem had never seen anything like it before: six stars to the left of the trunk, six to the right, with an additional one in the heart of the tree.

Suspicious, he had asked the craftsman for an explanation. After all, the Jerusalem-trained rabbi reasoned, trade routes from the Roman world snaked around the very base of the Nazareth Mountains. At night, when the wind was up, caravan songs could be heard as far as the village. Strange ideas would not have far to travel. How easily some sort of syncretism might insinuate itself among these people, exposed to Gentile influences and deprived of the guidance of scholars.

Joseph had turned his inscrutable gray eyes on the young rabbi. "Rabbi, I'm surprised. Really, you don't see it?" With a gentle laugh, he traced his finger along the outline of the design.

"The tree, of course, is the Torah," he explained. "The twelve tribes of Israel, the stars gathered around it."

"But there are thirteen stars here," the rabbi pointed out, more concerned than ever. "And thirteen is...," the rabbi chose his words carefully, "an unhappy number."

Joseph looked pleased. "Can it be that a poor country oaf like me has managed to outwit a scholar?"

The rabbi could not help smiling now himself.

"Twelve stars, the twelve tribes of Israel, and the thirteenth star—the Messiah," Joseph explained.

The rabbi muttered the ritual response. "May his coming be in our days."

"Amen. As you can see, I've put his star there—the Messiah's star—in the heart of the oak, in the Torah's heart."

"Still, my friend," the rabbi persisted, "the number thirteen is unfortunate."

"Thirteen," Joseph said, rolling up the scroll, "a star for his sufferings."

The rabbi, though, could not shake off a sense of unease. Such luxuriant designs would never do for a Judean synagogue, he thought. The whole business had a slightly pagan air about it. After all, there was the Torah's prohibition against graven images to worry about.

In the days that followed, Joseph continued his efforts to reassure the rabbi of Nazareth. And soon the freshly sculpted surfaces of the Nazareth synagogue were alive with pelicans and cranes, rushes and badgers, with peacock tails trailing down the sides of columns, and, exploding from every corner, pomegranate trees, date palms and grape arbors.

But, far more than the synagogue project, what had really brought the two men together was Miriam. How could Menachem ever forget the day when Joseph told him of his intention to marry her?

Miriam! Menachem's wife Ruth had been the one to point her out to him shortly after their arrival in the hamlet. Clear-eyed, sober, possessed of a cultivated, almost delicate beauty, the girl, Ruth observed, was "like a pearl hidden in the shell of these hard, black hills."

The grinding poverty of life here at the borders of the Roman world seemed to crush the spirits of Nazareth women early. Before they were twenty, childbirth and sickness had taken their toll on even the sturdiest of them. But not this one, not Miriam. Though saddled with an orphan's life, living with a houseful of particularly disagreeable relatives after the death of her elderly parents, Miriam seemed to bear everything with grace and wit, utterly unbowed, apparently oblivious to the dark world of bitter gossip and envy which so marked the landless scratch-poor of Galilee.

"There is music," Ruth observed, "in the very way she holds her head."

...Jewish husbands,

Menachem's pen continued to run over the parchment contract,

> *who work for their wives, honoring*
> *and supporting them....*

Menachem could still feel the sudden blow in the pit of the stomach administered the day when Joseph came to tell him, in a dead man's voice, that Miriam, his betrothed, was pregnant—and that he was not the father.

The village had not been easy on either of them.

Most had expected the builder to marry someone from Kefar Kana. That was the thing for a man of Joseph's gifts, Joseph's potential, to do.

But Miriam, Simon of Clopas' ward? It was beyond belief that Joseph would marry into that clan! Of course, everyone was aware that the contractor was distantly related to them, but there were dozens of Davidic families in Galilee to choose from. Why go with that brood of vipers?

Simon of Clopas and his sons: dirt poor and crafty as weasels, parading their once-noble ancestry for every ignoble gain. The elder of the clan, it was said, was on a continual campaign to "milk" locals of their meager cash, if not through outright swindles, then through squeezing out loans on the basis of the family's pedigree and allegedly vast land holdings in Judea. Naturally, you couldn't get a shekel out of them later.

Even the rabbi had had to admit that while Miriam herself seemed a perfect match for his friend, the family worried him. "They're such a volatile, unpopular tribe," he'd complained to his wife. But he had never foreseen a development like this.

The two men hiked into the fields outside the village—fields which allowed them a modicum of relief from Nazareth's ever-prying eyes and ears. They sat down in the shade of a Tabor oak on the top of the ridge, Joseph's favorite spot for thinking.

"Strange," said Joseph, his nerves at last under control. "It was here that I decided to marry her." He leaned his head back against the tree.

"It was night," he reminisced, "and the stars shone as they do only on the tops of mountains. I was troubled about the prospect of marrying Miriam—troubled about *my* worthiness, not hers. But then I looked up into the black heavens. Does anything in this vast army of the sky resist the will of its maker, I asked myself? No, the Blessed One has but to speak the word and all creation answers: Here I am!

"I felt as if a door in the universe had opened, as though I'd crossed some sort of frontier, a new country from which I could never return..." Joseph's voice faltered.

Menachem slowly edged into what was for him, the rabbi of Nazareth, the most pressing question: Did Joseph have any idea who the culprit was? Obviously, once Miriam's condition became known, everyone would assume that Joseph had "soiled his own bed" as the saying went. But Menachem knew his friend.

He pressed his inquiry. If the builder had heard something, suspected something.... A Nazarene offender would quickly divide the village into warring camps, knives would be drawn. The jocular, easy-going Galileans had a reputation for ferocity when it came to "family" issues.

Of course, there was always the possibility that the girl had been assaulted on one of the outlying roads by a stranger or, God forbid, a Roman soldier, Menachem mused. Simon of Clopas was, after all, known to be cozy with the commander of the garrison at Sepphoris.

Naturally, he'd not spoken with Miriam herself, Joseph said in reply. And then, after a very long silence, the builder recounted the half-coherent rumors circulating among the Clopas women—that Miriam had had "a visitation of angels."

"Angels don't beget children," Menachem had snapped, furious with himself now for advising the match and anxious about the ruin Miriam's transgression would surely bring on his hapless friend, and perhaps the village too.

"You must divorce her—quietly," Menachem said finally. "Don't worry. I'll see to it that she's sent away somewhere."

The warm night wind came up over the Nazareth Mountains, rippling the poplars outside the House of Study where the young rabbi sat putting the finishing touches on the final marriage contract between Joseph, son of Jacob, and Miriam, daughter of the priest Joachim.

...Jewish husbands,

he wrote carefully,

who maintain their wives...in truth.

He looked over his work. As he sat examining the letters

one by one in the dimming lamplight, he could smell the faint odor of the Sea of Galilee in the sudden windrise.

The couple's second contract was finished.

(The scribe found himself wondering about the rumor he'd heard: that Joseph had had the first document—the one drafted for their engagement, the one written before the troubles came—buried like a stillborn child in the earth at the foot of the oak tree.)

Menachem sat back in the cool stone rabbi's seat. He entertained a secret satisfaction in the recesses of his heart that Joseph had ignored his advice and taken responsibility for the child and the bride before the council of elders. Miriam was fortunate to have betrothed the one man in Galilee for whom loyalty was everything.

Still, in the end, it was Joseph that troubled him most. This whole business of the drawing up of a second marriage contract was highly unusual. And all these special conditions the man had insisted on adding to the text! Of course, Menachem reminded himself that Galileans were known to be fond of these extra-legal elaborations: there were the stipulations that, if possible, the couple would reside forever in the land of Israel. That was a harmless enough insertion. And "seeking the special blessedness of the lowly"—well, that too had a certain Galilean charm.

But what was this business about "agreeing to live for the Messiah, Son of David our ancestor, and to shelter, guard and defend his coming?"

Menachem's musings were broken by a knock at the door. That would be the young couple, he said to himself, putting aside his disquiet long enough to prepare to greet them with a cordial if slightly official smile.

31

TALE OF THE
ROMAN CROSS

He didn't need to be told that this was the place. Even in the darkness, there was the aroma of death, the whisper of faint, belabored breathing, the kind of stillness that is itself a sound.

The reek of wet fertile soil permeated the predawn Galilee, creating a cruel counterpoint to the slow, invisible dance of the crucified.

As Baruch crouched in his hiding place beside the lake road locals called "the Ring," impressions assailed one another in his mind. It was as if his physical senses, confronted with the reality of death, had never been more alive.

A keen farmboy's nose informed him that a record wheat crop was in the offing this year on the Golan. A certain indefinable earth smell in the weeks before spring told you that. His father surely was already calculating the profits.

Well, perhaps not now. Not since Zvi. Not since yesterday. His father would think of nothing now except to rage at his one surviving son. Baruch, after all, was to blame.

He felt for the package at his side. The narcotic was still there. And his long trusty double-edged, just in case.

How long had it been since he had enjoyed the homey rituals of a farmer's life? Ever since Judas the Galilean had inducted him and his brother Zvi into the *kananayeh*—the ones the Greek-speakers call "Zealots"—peaceful preoccupations had become a luxury.

"Farming—that's a pursuit for free men," the revolutionary had remarked when Zealot recruiters failed at first to pry the two brothers from their livelihood. "Isn't that a Roman heelprint I see on your brow?" Judas had focused his words like a spear. "I wouldn't call *you* free."

But the farmboys had proved able guerrillas. The keen sense of terrain and weather bequeathed to the brothers by forebears had stood them in good stead more than once in their exploits as highwaymen.

To pinpoint the precise whereabouts of far-off sounds, to understand the language of bird cries—this was essential if one were to make one's living being a professional "scourge of Romans."

Not that Baruch could claim to be in his younger brother's league. Zvi's eye, even in pitch dark, was uncanny. It was said by fellow revolutionaries that Zvi, "the Deer," could sense Roman soldiers coming even when scouts failed to spot them.

A bitter piece of irony! That very hero-worship had led directly to Zvi's capture. His youthful band, inured to success, cocky, overconfident—they'd not even spied the patrol until it was on top of them. As for the quick-witted "Deer": he was curled up in a corner of the cave, asleep.

Zvi! The name now tasted like blood in his mouth.

Baruch checked the small linen bag once again. The rag and the vial were inside. The mixture called myrrh—grains of laudanum laced with wine—the assurance of a painless death. How did the Galilean folksaying go:

> *While the body dies like a beast,*
> *the mind is a lion freed....*

They've had plenty of practice in these parts, he thought to himself. It's been a mere two years since Varus, "the Butcher," Roman governor of Syria, had seen fit to impress the Roman Senate with his devotion to the imperial cause by planting forests of crucified Jews along these roads.

34

He could smell the slightly balsamic scent of the myrrh rising from his satchel.

Your robes are all fragrant with aloes and myrrh.

Like a cruel joke, the words from the Wedding Psalm rose to his lips. Myrrh once graced the robes of Jewish kings, he mused darkly. A sign of the times surely that now we employ it to relieve the pains of those crucified like slaves!

Baruch didn't notice the woman at first when he crept up over the rocks at daybreak, moving like a lynx toward the row of dark figures projected against the blue backdrop of the Golan.

He'd been waiting all night for the caravan to pass this way, for its lumbering wagons to shield from Roman eyes a rebel's attempt to reach a dying brother.

But the enemy was not patrolling heavily tonight. After all, the caravans were Jewish—safe, presumably, from the predatory Zealots. And why should Romans interfere with Jews traveling to register for a Roman census? Still, the wagons should reduce the risk, Baruch had calculated. He was an outlaw, after all.

It made him sick to watch these Galileans straggle like pack animals to pay their Roman taxes: the "Chosen People" submitting meekly to their captors, paying for the Roman plunder of their lands. Had they not become architects of their own collective prison, pawning the birthright of the "sons of God" to become—like other nations—the docile stooges of dark, ignorant powers?

"A veil of illusion has fallen over the people's mind," his Zealot mentor had once told him. "They really don't *see*, Baruch."

He had only to recall his last argument with his father. "When the Messiah comes to set you free," he had fumed at its end, "you'll probably tell him not to bother."

"Something like that," his father had replied, indulgently. "When the Messiah comes, I'll still have to prune my olive trees."

The knot of wagons and travelers thickened on the surface of the muddy road. Baruch made his move, easing himself into the confusion.

Women, conscious of the dying men on crosses at the side of the road, were bustling the younger children out of sight. A few of the men, eyes averted, attended to their wagons and murmured prayers for the dying as they passed.

Strangely, Baruch, still edging his way through the crowd, saw the woman even before his eyes took in the tortured figure of his brother.

She looked to be about fifteen. Heavy with child, she was perched on a donkey, daubing the face of the dying Zealot with her veil, murmuring something, or so it seemed, into the gaping features of that once-beautiful face.

That face—only the now-huge child's eyes seemed still alive, following the movement of the woman's lips as though they breathed the warmth of suns.

Baruch stood still as stone before the scene, unable to draw closer, oddly afraid of intruding. Zvi's once-lithe, animal-swift frame had been beaten past recognition; its familiar contours replaced now by a landscape of lesions and sores. The smell of urine assaulted the man's nostrils as he forced himself forward.

Shame, too, assailed him. The Romans had been known to do terrible things to those who were caught commiserating with their victims. Even a cup of cold water or a whispered blessing might bring down the full weight of their wrath.

Yet this woman, this daughter worthy of the Maccabees, stood there openly under a Roman sky performing her pieties. He, Baruch, on the other hand, the "Roman Killer," lurked in the shadows like a thief.

A figure approached the woman—her husband surely—leading her gently away and out of danger, back into the safety of the caravan. The Zealot's keen eye could not help but notice the Bethlehem star sewn on the sleeve of the man's garment. So, they were members of the royal house, Baruch reasoned, on their way no doubt to Bethlehem, and she, with child. "May such a bride be found worthy of the Promised One," he muttered under his breath, edging forward.

He fumbled into the darkness of his satchel for the myrrh. And with the dark face of his brother looming above him, he hoisted a drug-soaked rag on his double blade.

Mercifully, for Baruch, suddenly fearful of the moment of recognition, Zvi's eyes were closed. The reek of the myrrh swirled under the nostrils of the fallen rebel. After what seemed a very long time, his eyes blinked open. Slowly recognizing the remedy that lay against his lips, he forced a swollen tongue over the sponge and drank.

Baruch was radiant, sensing the dawn of recognition. "*Achi*...brother...."

Zvi's face grew animated. His eyes tried to focus. After several attempts, he finally choked the words out of his slowly collapsing lungs: "Bar...(a)ba(s)...."

Baruch's head sank. It was "vintage Zvi"—Zvi to the last. The "name rhymes" they had made up as children: "You may be the 'Deer' (swift), but I'm Baruch ('lucky')."

"Barabbas"—the slightly reproachful "father's boy"—it had always been Zvi's favorite nickname for his older brother. Now, a brave, whimsical farewell at the gates of death.

That year nature proved far kinder to Baruch than the Romans. The bumper wheat crop on the Golan, which he had predicted, more than materialized. The harvest, in fact, was so fruitful that farmers had to hire extra hands from the Decapolis to gather it.

Baruch alone remained aloof from this abundance until his wife delivered a son that spring—their first-born.

In his brother's memory, he named him Barabbas.

TALE OF THE
KEY OF DAVID

It took no time at all for Bethlehemites to arrive at a nickname for the thousands of guests who had descended upon them for the Roman census—*chagabim*, "locusts."

Even the oldest Bethlehemite could not remember a time when such mobs choked the town's narrow streets. Even Passover, when Bethlehem filled with extended family members come for the holy days in nearby Jerusalem, was not like this. The agora, the large open-air market on the eastern edge of the town, had become a tent city. Residents could hardly get to their own doorways, finding squatters encamped along every stretch of wall. And the dust all this unruly mob and their animals raised!

Ordinarily, townspeople could have expected to have such discomforts assuaged somewhat by the amount of business the crowds would bring in their wake. No such luck. The thousands who blanketed the town were, after all, family. "Each man is to return to his own birthplace," the Roman order read, "to be registered for purposes of taxation." The rules of oriental hospitality forbade accepting even a token payment for services rendered to relatives, however distant. "Leave it to the Romans," Bethlehemites muttered, "to plunder us by means of our own brothers."

But whatever the particular provocation, Bethlehem's year-round population of 900 had a reputation for being "touchy" in any case. Their Jerusalem "cousins" seven miles to the north regaled dinner parties with jokes at Bethlehem's expense, poking merciless fun at the townsfolk's fabled sense of wounded dignity, their stubborn pride and the Bethlehem miserliness which sometimes, in reality, assumed epic proportions.

It had ever been thus, the Bethlehem-Jerusalem rivalry.

Bethlehem had once figured as Judea's most impressive urban site, several hundred feet higher on the Judean plateau than the nearby Jebusite fortress town of Jerusalem. In ancient times, when Bit-Lahmi had rebelled against Ursalim's tyranny, reinforcements had to be summoned all the way from Egypt in order to subdue the city.

Sitting atop its craggy mountain, Bethlehem's springs made the sloping hillsides a paradise of olive groves and vineyards, its plains a vista of wheat. (By contrast, Bethlehemites were eager to point out, Jerusalem's forbidding terrain had little water and was utterly useless for farming.) Little wonder then the ancients called Bethlehem *Ephrata*, Bethlehem the Fruitful.

Today, Bethlehem was little more than a picturesque rural suburb of metropolitan Jerusalem, its smallish population living close to the cypress-wooded hilltop where the town had originally been founded, huddled around the ruins of greatness long past and of the still more potent memories of its ancestral heroes. Bethlehemites still sang the haunting folk songs about *Immanu Rachel*—"Rachel Our Mother"—who had died giving birth to Benjamin, the patriarch, beside Ephrata, and did the dizzy "wheat reaping dances" in honor of the marriage of Ruth and Boaz each spring.

No one, however, was buried so deep in Bethlehem's collective affections as the king the town had given to the nation: David, son of Jesse.

And through David, the promise of future greatness still lay. Had not the Prophet written of Bethlehem: "And you, Bethlehem-Ephrata, least among the tribes of Judah, from you shall come forth the [future] ruler of Israel"? Bethlehem would deliver yet another "David" to the nation, promised the Sacred Writings; this one, the "Deliverer" himself. "Let the Romans tax us then until we can barely scratch a living out of soil rich as clay," the townspeople groused behind closed doors, "let Jerusalem's 'progressives' strut about like Greeks and drink out of alabaster goblets. Our day will come."

"We are the Key of David," sang Bethlehem's children on Passover night, "the key that unlocks the Messiah's door."

So far so good, she thought to herself. She had managed to get the key off the peg without anyone seeing her. By the time anyone misses it...but, perhaps, in all the bustle, no one will miss it at all.

Maacah wrapped the heavy wool mantle about her as she slipped silently into the street. Good, she thought, the light's fading fast. Still, the chances of making her way completely unobserved through the city where she had lived all her life were slim at best. All she could hope for was that everything could be prepared quickly, before anyone had a chance to stop her.

There was no doubt in her mind what her relatives would make of her actions—taking a delicate family matter into her hands like this. Brazen, some would call it.

No, the women of the Davidic clan were not educated to take bold action in the public forum. Their strengths lay elsewhere—not in the breezy world of politics and piety, the domain of their menfolk—but inside them: in the silent steel of hope, in the fierce quiet of an indomitable will.

Maacah felt for the key. Yes, it was there, tied firmly to her belt. That strange iron key that had fascinated her since childhood. She could still see her grandfather Shimon—may his soul rest with the righteous—sitting on a stool, just before he went to wash for Evening Prayer, holding up the key with its leaf-like handles to the light of the setting sun.

Sitting at his feet, his favorite granddaughter would observe how the design of the old key divided the multi-colored sky into windows of indescribable hue. Should a flock of swallows happen to whiz by, he would inform her that they were the ink of the Messiah's secret inscriptions, glimpsed only out of the corner of an eye when the light is almost gone, written on the surface of the wind.

One day, when she was older—shortly before he died, in fact—the old man took her aside. "Did you ever think, child, that there was a reason behind the game of the key we played when you were little?" he inquired, oddly serious. "No," she had replied. "It was just child's play, Grandfather, wasn't it?" "Oh, no," he smiled, waiting to see if he had her full attention. "There was much more to it than that," he said. "The game of the key was to teach you that everything points to the Messiah—everything exists for him. You must learn to listen in all the sounds around you for his footsteps."

"Why, Grandfather?" she had countered. "Surely the Messiah will come with his legions. Everyone will know."

"On the contrary, child. He will come like a flock of swallows across the sky, in the time it takes for twilight to pass into evening, as sudden as"—he had paused again—"the sound of a key in the lock." They had both laughed.

And yet, after that, she'd always insisted on getting out the key to her grandfather's house during the yearly Passover games, brandishing the antique whenever the children sang the refrain about the "Key of David."

Maacah clattered down the long stepped slope from the market square, doing her best to melt into the milling waves of late-arriving pilgrims. A watchman had already shouted the dreaded warning that Bethlehem's gates would soon close for the night, leaving stragglers to fend for themselves outside the city until morning. Vulnerable to plundering by raiders, confidence men and the packs of wild dogs which scavenged after dark, the unfortunates could be heard brawling for squatters' rights to the safest spots near the gates.

The air was full of the sounds of braying animals and their shouting owners. At nightfall, bursting at the seams with its human burden, Bethlehem seemed less like a city than one huge discontented child, alive only to the chaos of its collective urgencies.

A sea of faces met Maacah as she descended into the city's dense old quarter. But, imposed on the nameless crowd, she saw the features of her beloved grandfather and those of Joseph, blended by her mind into a strange composite.

Not so strange, though, the girl reasoned. "It's only because of my grandfather that I'm willing to go through with this crazy errand," something tightened inside of her. "Joseph has him to thank that I'm having anything to do with him at all." She was steeling herself to tell him just that when she spied the small dome of her grandfather's house behind the sprawling caravanserai and the dark knot of shadows behind it which hid the cave.

Did the flickering light in the darkness mark where her fallen cousin stood waiting, she wondered? Would *she* be there, his bride, the one who had disgraced him? Would Joseph say anything? What could he say? After all, his tumble from grace had wounded Maacah most of all. Surely, someone had informed him about that by now.

His face, the face of Yochanan her betrothed, filled Maacah's eyes. How would she ever forget the terrible confusion on that youthful countenance as he announced to her father that an engagement was out of the question. Her family's hopes for a "Jerusalem connection" undone, their prospects waylaid by the sordid tales from the north.

"You can't expect the Yehuda Ben-Aaron's, a priestly clan, to marry into a family which permits...." Maacah had been unable to bear any more of the discussion.

To make matters worse, Joseph, once the family's pride, was silent; not a word of remorse or explanation, not a hint of extenuating circumstances—nothing.

For this reason, Maacah's father, knowing that Joseph and his bride would be journeying to Bethlehem for the census, forbade any member of the family to so much as greet them. "This man dishonors not only us," he had shouted, "but our ancestor King David himself—may his memory be blessed. Joseph has apparently forgotten whose blood runs in his veins. Well, forgetfulness begets forgetfulness. Let him find housing for himself like a stranger. No one is to so much as speak to the man, do you hear? Not a word!"

Maacah, however, had not been able to forget her grandfather's admonition. "Trust Joseph always," these had been his deathbed words to her.

She paused before disappearing into the shadows of her grandfather's house, assuming the grim demeanor with which she thought it appropriate to greet her cousin. The eyes of the alleyways' many strangers followed her. Grandfather's manger, she thought—it must be the last uninhabited spot in the city.

A figure approached her as she reached the doorway to the grotto. It was not a stranger. A light from the inn suddenly illumined his face. With a start, Maacah observed, for the first time, that Joseph had the beautiful gray eyes of her grandfather. Why had she never noticed this before?

Silently, without a word, she handed her cousin the ancient key.

TALE OF THE
ALABASTER JAR

T he woman's gaze met his. Afterwards, he had found himself unable to describe precisely what it was about the young mother's look that had affected him so deeply. Nevertheless, under the shelter those dark, graced eyes afforded, the old magus realized quite suddenly that he had come to a decision.

"Tell all the attendants to leave," he murmured to his Abyssinian aide. "But, Eminence...," the slave hesitated. The magus—"Eye of the Universe" they called him in Babylon—stared down at the mother and child seated before him. "Do as I say," he said gently.

The young Abyssinian ushered the small company of eminent magi, disciples, servants and guards out of the cramped, musty room. Mild protests could be heard, especially from the other magi, as they regrouped outside in the cold night air of the Judean highlands. "A 'Night of Revelation'," they whispered incredulously, "and great masters are not to be present? For what purpose, then, have we accompanied the priest Asshur all the way from Babylon if not to aid in the discernment of the prophecies and portents pertaining to the child? Is Asshur alone wise?"

The Abyssinian tried to calm them. "Hold your tongues," he said, pulling his great gold-embroidered cloak about him. "I'm sure the Eminence will explain himself shortly."

But the Abyssinian himself had to admit that he could not fathom what was in the master's mind. Past excursions to tell the fortunes of great world leaders had always been highly public affairs. When great Asshur's grandfather, the magus

Aristobolus, had attended the birth of Mithridates—also announced by a star—there had been more than a week of sacrifices at which dozens of magi had assisted, consulting the omens. Precise records had been kept of everything that had transpired.

"Could it be that Asshur is...uncertain?" The thought, unspoken, crossed the Abyssinian's mind. "He has slept badly since we pitched our tents outside the gates of Bethlehem." Asshur of Babylon, the world's reigning expert on the mystical properties of plants, tossing in his sleep like a witless camel-driver?

In any case, it was uncomfortable for the master's party to remain exposed like this in the immediate vicinity of the house, the Abyssinian muttered to himself. The arrival of such eminent foreigners had sparked the curiosity of the whole town. Large numbers of onlookers had been milling about the house for days. The child's relatives had practically taken up residence around the young couple, inquiring constantly about the strangers' visit, disturbing the quiet essential to the performance of a magus' intricate undertakings.

To avoid all this, some of the younger magi had proposed removing the child and his mother to the safety and comfort of their encampment just outside the city. It would be easier to examine them there, free of the nuisance of the townspeople and King Herod's ubiquitous spies. The child's parents, however, had politely but firmly declined the offer.

It had reached the Abyssinian's ears that, before their arrival, the wonder-child and his parents had been practically outcasts in the town, shunned even by their own family. Well, the slave noted to himself, warming his gold-ringed hands over a brazier, that had certainly changed. Their family these days was acting the very soul of consideration.

A nondescript-looking bunch for the remnants of a Judean royal house, the Abyssinian couldn't help but observe. "It's sad to find a fabled clan reduced to this—to behaving like a gang of vulgar profiteers," he had confided to one of the magus' aides. "And without so much as a shred of wit or subtlety—any of them."

King Herod was surely right to conclude that the likes of these posed no great threat to his throne.

The light from clay lamps inside the house created a map of shadows across the rough limestone walls. The child was asleep, wrapped in layers of silence like the linen cloths which swaddled him. The father, similarly engulfed in the warm tent of his prayer shawl, muttered the cadences of *Ma'ariv*, the Evening Prayer, from the dim-lit recess of the room. Asshur listened as the patter of syllables rolled off the young man's tongue, each one precise as a jewel.

> *Blessed are you, O Lord our God, King of the Universe,*
> *who at your word brings on the twilight,*

the man recited,

> *with wisdom opens the gates of the heavens,*
> *and with understanding changes times and varies seasons,*
> *and arranges the stars in their watches in the sky....*

A child born in a cave, Asshur reflected. He had ascertained this important fact the very first day after the arrival in Bethlehem. It was his business to understand the meaning of such incidentals—the metaphysical landscape of events, as he told his students. Caves—lowest plane of existence, the place farthest removed from the realm of light, closest to the kingdom of darkness: into just such a place, the child had dawned.

Had not the ancients divided the cosmos into eight descending realms:

> The World of Lights
> and The Firmament,
> The Worlds of The Mountain,
> The Saint,
> The Man,
> The Book,
> The Earth
> and The Cave?

What does it mean, then, he reasoned, when the process is reversed: when light dawns in a cave, when great kings, heralded by stars, are born in squalor? Has God overturned his own universe? The mind of the old scholar reeled. The only thing about which one could be sure in Bethlehem was that all lay hidden, removed from the calculations of men. The dreams of a dozen sleepless nights had taught him that: great bronze doors shut tight against all his magic. Knowledge itself, it seemed, had no pride of place in the new universe born in a cave.

The woman continued to watch the sage in silence as he slowly drew out the small alabaster jar from its dark velvet case. Without a word, Asshur placed the marble vessel before him and knelt on the cool beaten earth before the sleeping child.

The woman smiled.

Asshur stroked the smooth carved surface of the casket, resisting for a moment the difficult deed he knew he must perform.

The myrrh jar: what a pedigree it had! Bequeathed to

Asshur by his father, research had failed to locate the magician who had once had it scooped out of the purest marble. Marble, the fruit of limestone, the rock closest to the element of water, source of all life. As a magic vessel, it had once so long ago been used to anoint the feet of the hero Mithridates, its worn soap-smooth surface covered with enchantments.

Intoning the blessing reserved for kings under his breath, the Babylonian broke the jar's imposing wax seal, releasing into the hovel's four corners an aroma reserved only for the nostrils of gods.

The woman's face grew quietly grave, uncertain of the meaning of the strange ceremony. She turned to her husband who, having finished his prayers, came to join her before the kneeling sage.

The magus was silent, searching his mind. The mere smell of the aromatic spice was known to unlock the powers of prophecy.

No use. Could it be that such demonstrations were already a thing of the past? Could it be that the powers now lay slumbering not in the tireless manipulations of wise men, but in a pauper's dreams?

Such prophecy as the moment warranted was in the act he was about to perform.

With a trembling hand, the old man shattered the sacred alabaster jar, prize of the Babylonian academies, on the stone-hard earth before the mother and child. Perfume flooded the dark recesses of the room as the old man contemplated the pile of broken shards at his feet. His hands dripping with myrrh, Babylon's greatest magus, with strokes of infinite tenderness, anointed the five senses of the sleeping infant.

The woman's eyes searched his for an explanation. The child's father rushed to help the old man to his feet.

52

But Asshur's task was not quite finished.

Strange, unfamiliar words were forming on his tongue. Reeling in the myrrh-intoxicated air, the magus performed, as it turned out, the final magic deed of his career, the career of Asshur, last of the true magi.

"I have anointed your son for the trials of his manhood," he prophesied. "You must tell him this when he is of the age of understanding. When another breaks the jar before him," the old man said, "he will know that the hour for which he was born...is at hand."

The sage's hand fluttered in the air as he performed there in the damp hovel the obeisances rendered to kings, and, slowly withdrawing, caught once more a glimpse of the woman's look of inexhaustible wonder.

TALE OF THE
TESTAMENT

H erod insisted on being carried straight to his bath after the long and painful journey from Jerusalem. Every jolt the royal litter had sustained on the trek down the dry desert valleys toward Jericho had jarred the increasingly brittle nerves of the King of the Jews. His head was hot with the fever that never seemed to leave him these days. Eczema covered the surface of his vast bloated frame. Even the sovereign's hands had been swaddled to prevent him from scratching himself raw.

Understandably, the king's excursions to Jerusalem were increasingly rare. If his doctors had their way, Herod would never have left his sprawling palace complex in lovely, temperate Jericho under any circumstances, with its proximity to rejuvenating hot springs and the sulphur baths of Callirrhoe.

But advisers also knew that even a Herod in agony could not afford to ignore the incessant challenges to his authority in the Holy City, challenges which swirled about the aging ruler like carrion birds.

This particular excursion had palace tongues wagging: A top secret interview with some Babylonian metaphysicians, it was said. Aides to Nathan of Gaza, Herod's trusted adviser, were reporting that the king had secured from the foreigners some sort of magic formula to restore his youth. "Had Herod not prophesied that they would find him one day with skin as smooth as an infant's?"

Attendants rushed to bundle the king out of his conveyance, careful to avoid the old man's glance. They knew only too well that when the sick old king was in pain, his cruel temper was especially capricious. One false move, one clumsy gesture....

But Herod the Great was preoccupied at the moment: He was trying to breathe. The massive torso slumped against the carriage, his chest heaved and sputtered with wheezing. It took three slaves to lift the half-conscious ruler into the palace toward the steaming baths which alone offered some measure of relief from his multiple afflictions.

Splendid frescoes of the heroic exploits of Hercules and Perseus looked down on the body of the reclining Jewish king, now wide awake, bathed in steam, after the day's grueling journey. Sitting in a huge throne-like tub in his tepidarium, his nostrils graced with the smell of fragrant oils, the king was sufficiently recovered from his pains to consider his next moves.

Heat had reddened his swath of sores to the point where the massive bulk of the monarch looked nearly like another patch of the bright tempera paint on the bathhouse wall, his swollen figure a mockery of the athletic torsos brandishing their golden swords above him.

Herod leaned his head back with difficulty, vaguely musing for a moment on the lean figures painted at his command by an expert Greek artist. He too had been an athlete in his youth, the equal of any Roman javelin thrower. In fact, during his days with Mark Antony, he had been a better athlete than any of the other aristocrats in his circle. He'd had to be. He was, after all, a foreigner, an interloper, a man who'd had to prove himself at every turn.

The interloper—this had been his fate wherever he had found himself. He had been a mere Idumean for the Jewish royal house into which he had inserted himself by marriage—

a dynasty he had managed to outwit through his Roman connections. With his Roman patrons, he'd had to overcome their prejudice against Jews. And as for the Jews, did people really think he did not know the names they called him: Herod, the "Half-Jew," "Herod of [pagan] Ascalon," Herod, the "Edomite Slave"? Some of the Pharisees went so far as to refuse to utter his name at all, referring to him merely as "that man."

Fine. If he would not be loved, he could at least be well hated. And he had had the satisfaction of making his enemies pay dearly for their hatred.

Herod sighed as the steam untied the aching knot in his lungs. A Jewish king had need of the inspiration of pagan heroes. If he had not kept faith with Israel's God—and he had not—at least he had found it useful to keep faith with the likes of Hercules and Perseus: men full of ruthless self-interest and epic audacity in the face of the gods.

Audacity in the face of the gods—not a bad epitaph for himself, the old king mused.

Epitaphs. Yes, they were all waiting, circling like crows, for Herod the Great to die.

The rabbis of Jerusalem, he was sure, had already purchased wine for the celebration. The pious son, Antipater, Jerusalem's "favorite," paced anxiously in the wings. "Surely you know how dangerous it is to be impatient," Herod had warned him in a recent interview. Antipater's face had frozen. He would not soon forget the fate of his half-brothers Alexander and Aristobolus, who had been strangled in their baths a year ago, attempting, it was charged, to hasten their father's end.

Even God, it appeared, could hardly wait for death to swallow him. Long dormant, the House of David was on the rise again. Herod might be considered irreligious, but he was not without respect for the supernatural. The magi from Babylon had been very persuasive. Clearly, Bethlehem had produced a secret Davidic heir, and the signs pointed to divine approval.

Well, the old fox smiled, two can play at this game.

Had not the Roman sibyl so many years ago promised a restoration of his youth on the very point of death? Like Hercules, Herod would gamble the work of a lifetime on one last wager—and this one against the King of Kings.

Herod clapped his hands. The attendant sped into the bathhouse, falling on one knee before him. "Tell Nathan to come to me," he said hoarsely. "Tell him to bring the Will."

Archelaus had been sick already twice that morning, anticipating the afternoon interview with his father. He had informed his mother that he intended to flee to the coast. But she had dissuaded him from this disastrous course of action. "If you leave now, his torturers will take it out on me," Malthace had cried.

Palace gossip had it that the king had asked last night for the Will—Herod's testament, the legal document of the succession—to be sent on to the Emperor Augustus for ratification. Archelaus knew well that the crazy old man had frequently revised it, on the whim of the moment, debasing one heir, elevating another, tacking on secret addenda to the document, disinheriting members of the family or secretly ordering their "removal."

What had happened, Archelaus pondered? Had Antipater accused him of conspiracy? Had Philip, his brother? Was old Nathan, Herod's adviser, up to something?

The brow of the young prince gleamed with sweat as he was brought in to face his father. The old man's eyes were only half open as he lay under the ministry of a muslin robe soaked in hot oil. Cysts had just been lanced on the king's thighs and the room reeked of their odors.

Archelaus stood there for what seemed an eternity before his father's bloodshot eyes fastened upon him.

"Antipater has refused my request," Herod croaked.

Archelaus could not keep a broad smile from creeping across his face. Relief swept over him like a cascade of cool water. Nobody had accused him of anything. On the contrary, Herod wanted something.

"How could a loyal son resist his father's wishes?" the prince said, his muscles relaxing.

"My testament is my will," the king growled, watching Archelaus' every move.

The prince understood at once. It was a loyalty test. The succession depended on carrying out Herod's orders to the letter. Antipater, the heir apparent, had failed. Archelaus knew that such golden opportunities came but once in this treacherous family. Herod would not live long enough perhaps to alter the Will again. The prince's heart pounded. Doubtless, it was some horror his father wanted done, something conceived out of the blackness of his soul and his unceasing pain.

Herod, his strength exhausted, had no more words left in him. The all-powerful Nathan informed Archelaus of the task at hand. In Bethlehem of Judah, he was to conduct inquiries about the birth of a certain child. He was to be careful, but no pains were to be spared ascertaining its identity. Once the child was located, the prince was to await further instructions.

Archelaus nodded. The tall, gaunt Nathan paused a moment before he added, "It's a contest of wills." He looked straight at the prince. "Your eminent father has a most interesting conviction that he may, in fact, be able to hold the will of God...hostage, in a sense, in return for certain personal favors."

"What favors?" Archelaus asked.

"Let's just say, a life for a life."

TALE OF THE
THIRTY PIECES OF SILVER

The moon rose behind the Mount of Olives, carving the three valleys of Jerusalem out of the shadows like a sculptor. City dogs barked in the distance, and, from the wilderness beyond, hyenas bayed into the warm night air.

The Roman officer standing at the fork of the three valleys noted, with relief, that the roads tonight were free of travelers. A few small campfires pierced the darkness of the limestone caves above him. Shepherds, surely. The low jangle of sheep bells told him as much. Otherwise, thankfully, he was alone.

The centurion was off duty, unhelmeted, his rank and nationality cloaked by a long hooded burnoose. His Hebrew, though marked by an Alexandrian accent, was flawless. His knowledge of Jewish customs exhaustive. Only the Roman sword, hidden at his side, would have betrayed his identity as a pagan, a servant of his imperial majesty, the Emperor Augustus.

But the Roman was hardly on imperial business this night, standing alone at the intersection of the Kidron, Tyropoean and Ben-Hinnom valleys. It was the Holy City's mystical heart, the spot where the roads form the shape of the Hebrew letter *shin*, first letter of the name of the Most High. Here, long before King David chose the Jebusite fortress Ursalim as his capital, Abraham had met the mysterious priest-king Melchisedek, ruler of Salem, and paid him a vassal's tithe.

Unlike most Romans, who could care less about Jewish "superstitions," this officer knew the Torah and the traditions well. In fact, as a son of one the Pharisees call "God-fearers," he had been raised not to reverence the capricious gods of the

Roman pantheon but the God of Israel instead.

Not that his father had been particularly religious. An Alexandrian merchant with Roman citizenship, his business dealings had been with that city's numerous Jews. Conversion to Judaism with him had been largely a function of his professional ambitions. Nevertheless, he had secured Pharisee tutors for his sons, and made passing attempts to observe the commandments—the ones which were not too inconvenient, circumcision chief among these.

The Roman untied the knots on his belt, pulling out a small leather pouch. In his haste on leaving the Praetorium, he had not even taken the time to count the money. He weighed the pouch in his hand. It was heavy with silver. But Bedouins, he knew, had a reputation for nearly bottomless greed. What if he had not brought enough with him to secure the Kedarites' cooperation? If Katiz, their chieftain, refused him, there was no time, no time at all, he fretted, to improvise an alternate scheme. Had he not seen the order signed that very morning? Archelaus' aide had delivered it to the Praetorium personally. "Urgent Action Required," it had read. Naturally, the prince wanted Roman soldiers to do his dirty work.

But Archelaus was surely more to be pitied than censured. God knew what sort of game old Herod was playing with him. Had not the Emperor himself once observed that it was safer to be Herod's pig than his son?

"Thirty pieces of the best Temple silver," the Roman counted in the metallic-tinted moonlight. "Katiz will want more, I know he'll want more," he fumed. "They don't call him *Ya-Katiz*—'Bee Sting'—for nothing."

A cool night wind descended into the valleys, bringing with it the contrasting scents of wild sage from the hills and the city's reeking garbage, smouldering in heaps at the western end of the dry wash of Ben-Hinnom.

The place had an unsavory reputation despite its mystical links to the city's founding. The ancients had called it the "Valley of Desolation" or, more commonly, the "Valley of the Slaughter." There the Israelites had committed their gravest abominations in the centuries before the Exile, incinerating their first-born sons alive in order to expiate the harvest god Moloch.

When the exiles returned, they cursed the Ben-Hinnom valley, with its terrible associations, refusing to farm its fertile floor. Instead, they littered the terrain with every unclean thing, unrolling the fiery carpet of their refuse and the corpses of unknown strangers into its depths. No wonder itinerant preachers called the valley not Ben-Hinnom but Gehenna— hell—symbol of the pit where wicked souls are said to burn.

"Valley of the Slaughter," the Roman shuddered in the cooling air. "How apt." Had the Bedouin considered such things when he suggested this spot for a rendezvous? Was not Herod, racked with disease, preparing to sacrifice innocents to the Moloch of his unappeaseable appetite for power?

Suddenly, he thought of the Child. He had seen him only once when Archelaus had sent him to Bethlehem to ascertain his whereabouts. The clever prince knew, of course, that the Roman's impeccable "Jewish credentials" would ease the town's suspicions. The parents had volunteered little information, but their relatives had told him everything he needed to know.

He had made up his mind then and there to do all he could to shield the Child from Herod. A mysterious impulse in a way. He had not been able to explain it adequately to himself. After all, Roman officers were forbidden to meddle in the affairs of Herod's kingdom.

But strange dreams had plagued him ever since he had

placed his fingers on the Child's cheek that afternoon in Bethlehem. Those gray, oddly knowing eyes.

A heavily robed figure moved out of the shadows of the Potter's Field toward him. The Roman realized, with annoyance, that the man had been observing him from the rise of terrain for more than half an hour. He probably suspected some sort of trap, the centurion reasoned.

Katiz greeted him in the clearing with the leisurely honorifics of the desert.

The Roman ordered the Bedouin to cut short the obsequies. "We have no time," he said. "I've had the boy moved. But the troops will be moving on Bethlehem within the hour. Herod must suspect as much since the order specifically includes the surrounding towns."

The chieftain nodded. The centurion's intelligence sources were second to none. "You know the plan, right?" the officer continued. "The family is to be disguised as Kedarites and escorted by way of the Sorek Valley to the sea. At Gaza, I've arranged for them to join a caravan across the desert to Alexandria. Is that clear?"

The Bedouin nodded a second time. The two black-mantled figures stood motionless in the moonlight as the conversation paused before moving to the rub of their discussion.

"You'll forgive me, my friend, if I get straight to the point," the Roman said at last. "How much do you want?"

The Bedouin's gold teeth gleamed for a moment. "If you'll forgive me, Roman, I've been observing you for some time, and I've some idea what you're prepared to offer."

"Katiz, look! There's no time for bargaining. I'll give you thirty pieces of silver for your trouble. Nothing more." They knelt down, Arab-style in the dust, where the officer counted out the silver coins on the generous hem of the Bedouin's robe.

"Your money is very clean," the Bedouin remarked, seeing that the Roman offered to pay him in Temple currency. "Let's see," he went on, "thirty pieces of silver. That's the price of a slave, isn't it? Hardly a fitting recompense to save a king's life."

The Roman grew furious. But the Bedouin, holding up a hand to calm him, said evenly, "Your Emperor doubtless has his reasons for making this purchase." (The Roman shuddered. He had not had time to reflect that he was placing his reputation in the wily Bedouin's hands.) "And," the old man winked, "a King of the Jews cannot be worth much more to Augustus than a Roman slave."

The officer decided that, under the circumstances, it was safer not to reply to that crack. The "Sting," after all, had just indicated, in discreet Bedouin fashion, that he had accepted payment and, more importantly, responsibility for the Child's safety.

Pocketing the pouch, the Bedouin received without comment the officer's last instructions. Suddenly overcome with gratitude, the centurion bowed deeply to the desert tribesman. Even now, at this late hour, perhaps Herod's dread intentions could be subverted, he thought. Rumors would fly quickly that the Child and his family had fled. Perhaps, the children of Bethlehem could be spared after all.

As he left the clearing at the fork of the three valleys, the Bedouin turned. He had one final question for the Roman. "If there is trouble later," he said without emotion, "to whom shall I address my...difficulties?"

The Roman smiled. It was clear that he would be hearing

from this Bedouin again. There would be many favors to be granted.

"My name is Jairus," he spoke into the darkness. "Ask for the centurion Jairus."

"hy does the ring tell us stories of the Child?" Issa quizzed the old man when he had finished his tales.

"Well put, son," said Shukri. "You've understood a great deal already."

"But I *don't* understand, Baba!" Issa exclaimed.

"All right, all right," the merchant smiled. "The stories of the Child, as you call them, tell us about the mystery—not of one—but of every birth."

Issa rolled the words around gently in his mind.

"Every birth...."

"Yes, of course," Shukri went on. "Every nativity occurs in the dark. Every life leaps down from the skies. Every conception announces the creation of a world."

"But what does that mean, Baba?" Issa asked.

The old man turned his face away.

"It means...that fathers are powerless to prevent the suffering they foresee in the eyes of their children."

It was nightfall by the time the boy and the merchant reached the Convent of St. Parakletos the Fatherless. Evening shadows had long since cast their borders across the landscape of the city.

Hidden behind a stone wall and half-buried beneath the level of the street, locals called the place "Courtyard of the Lemon Trees," although there was only one of those left now, forlorn and untended, its roots twisted into the stonework of the courtyard's well.

"Wait here," Shukri told Issa as he went off to summon Father Anastasios from his supper.

Issa shivered. He'd never been in this neighborhood before. Shadows darkened the few kerosene-lit windows looking down on him from the courtyard's terrace—a convent once, but now abandoned to strangers and refugees.

Jerusalem at night, alone: There were bats hunting in the sea-black skies and packs of wild dogs lurking in far-off shadows at the edge of the desert. But more, much more: There were haunted wells, and there were ghouls!

Had not his grandmother once laced his sleep with her tales of the night-prowling ghouleh who lived in the abandoned house next to the mosque, her voice disguised—it was said—sometimes in the barking of dogs, sometimes in the voice of the moaning winds? Once caught in her terrible embrace, children could extricate themselves from peril only by solving her riddles.

Ghassan, Ghassan,
tell me, clever,

69

when the white gazelle
becomes twice a unicorn?

Issa's grandmother, fortunately, had supplied him with the answer to this particularly wicked puzzle.

First when the ghouleh rides her
like the winds:
O the night horse of the Prophet.

Or twice when the ghouleh weds her bones
with its silver blood:
O elixirs of the Sultan.

Only the proper response could save one from being swallowed alive by the insatiable harpy, although very clever boys had been known to escape from her clutches by flattery.

Fear gripped his insides like the opening of an invisible wound: fear of the night, fear of nothing in particular, fear of everything. It had always been like that, the boy mused: fear as long and deep as memory.

Shukri had often spoken to him about it. "Must you tremble at every sound?" the old man would ask, passing his hand over the boy's brow. "What is it that frightens you?"

There could be no answer to that question. Issa had known somehow from the earliest days of his childhood not to tell a living soul—not even the merchant—that what terrified him most in this world was the sound of his mother's stifled cries in the stillness of the night.

Issa withdrew into the relative safety of the shadows cast by the lemon tree, trying to steady himself for what promised to be a long night ahead. He felt dizzy, disoriented, as though his adventures had rendered him as airborne as the riddle's magic gazelle.

The clean, sharp smell of the fruit reassured him somehow. It made him think of tables with starched white cloths he'd seen in restaurants, decked out with a dozen fragrant dishes and covered with bowls of fresh cut lemons. It made him think of his mother and the hours he'd spent helping her rub lampblack off brass with the juice of many lemons.

The warmth in his stomach also defended him a little against the night and the chill. Shukri had insisted they pause in their wanderings at one of the city's curbside cafes. There in the steamy warm interior, thick lamb stew and plates of hot brown taboun bread and tea awaited them. Shukri had even let Issa taste the brandy the old man downed at the end of the meal.

"For night travelers," he said mysteriously.

Issa asked the old man what he meant. Shukri smiled and asked the boy if he'd never heard about Moslems and their "nights of God" when "the pious listen to the words of the Koran until the morning, waiting for knowledge."

Issa *had* heard of such things, vaguely. The mosque above his courtyard had once been a convent of dervishes, about whom were told many stories.

"Are we going to stay up all night, Baba?" Issa cried.

"Perhaps..." the old man teased.

"Issa, Issa, where are you, child?"

The sound of the tapping cane shook the boy out of his reverie.

Emerging from his hiding place in the lemontree shadows, he saw two dark figures standing next to a small door opposite the well.

"Well, where is he?" a voice growled. That must be Father Anastasios, Issa thought. The sacristan of the old convent sported a large bib tucked under his chin and was clearly unamused by this intrusion into one of his life's few pleasures. "Hold this," he barked, thrusting a lighted taper into the boy's hand as he joined them.

"Thank you, Abuna," said Shukri expansively, "you are very kind to accommodate us...."

"Don't waste my time, I've got guests," the sacristan sniffed as he pulled a large ring of keys out of his cassock.

Issa knelt down beside the door, the candle fluttering like a moth between his palms while the priest fumbled with the lock.

What was going to happen now? The boy wondered why had Shukri brought him to this strange neighborhood on the other side of the city. What could possibly await them beyond the narrow door? With each click of the bolt, the boy felt something loosen inside him.

After what seemed like a very long time, the last bolt snapped back.

A sigh escaped Shukri's lips, like the sigh Issa had heard only that afternoon when the old merchant first touched the mysterious scarab ring.

For a moment, no one moved.

Then the old man asked Issa to face him directly. "You must never tell anyone about this place," he said, with an edge to his voice. "Anyone."

Issa giggled, embarrassed by the old man's sudden severity. Perhaps Shukri was playing some sort of game with him.

"Issa," said Shukri, squatting down before the boy. "This is serious. You must promise."

Issa felt the warmth of the blind man's hands on his shoulders. He saw the way the merchant's lips parted slightly as if trying to taste the meaning of the boy's responses.

"I'm speaking to you now like a man," Shukri said, softening.

Issa felt a strange peace inside him, something clear as the sky, hard as stone. He nodded again—slowly this time.

"I promise."

The priest coughed in the shadows. "Ah," sighed Shukri as he reached into the darkness behind him to maneuver a wad of dinars into the cleric's thick-fingered hand.

Warm light unfolded in the room beyond the doorway.

"Come, son," said Shukri, bearing an old brass lamp. "Help me find some candles."

Not large, deepened by the womb of a scalloped dome and ending in a narrow alcove, the chamber revealed by the spreading glow of Shukri's lamp was clearly a chapel of some kind.

Issa, bearing a long dark taper, scurried about the precincts, lighting everything in sight. Soon, the dark corners of the vestibule had been flushed free of shadows. Even the lime-damp walls themselves were glowing.

Issa took a survey of his surroundings.

A wooden icon screen spanned the sanctuary where a bare stone altar stood. Behind, at the chapel entrance, a narrow wooden pulpit with stairs curved unsteadily, almost to the ceiling. There were a few choir stalls along the walls. In the floor before the altar, a marble gravestone with Greek writing on it had been laid. And silver icon lamps hung everywhere.

But it was not as though the place were abandoned—that Issa noticed right away. Though wearing a slightly threadbare look, the shrine was spotlessly clean, and there was a bowl of fresh flowers on the altar—cyclamen, he thought.

In most respects, it was identical to a hundred other

musty-with-limewash shrines in the city. But it did have one riveting feature.

It was what Issa's flame had first chanced upon when he entered the doorway, before Shukri had summoned him inside: a large fading fresco of a star-flecked oak tree filling nearly the whole of the concave surface of the sanctuary wall.

At first glance, it looked as if a giant tree were actually growing there through the floor.

And though the icon screen shielded some of the details from view, it didn't take Issa more than a moment to recognize the pattern: There on the walls of an obscure Jerusalem church, itself hidden beneath the city's streets, was the image on his ring, the oak with the thirteen symbol-laden stars.

By now, the emblem had become infused on the very fibers of his imagination.

"Baba, I've found something!" cried Issa.

"Yes," Shukri answered from the vestibule where he was attempting to light a small wood-burning stove. "The painting—it's like your ring."

"How did you know that, Baba?"

"Come," said Shukri to the boy, "there'll be time for that later. Help me get the fire going. We'll need its warmth," he said gently.

As Issa turned to help the merchant, he saw an old Greek nun enter the chapel through a side door. There was a cord of firewood in her arms.

"Ah," said Shukri, detecting the presence of a stranger, "that would be the custodian. Good evening, Sister Timothea."

How had the old man managed to hear her, Issa wondered? She hadn't made a sound. The extraordinary delicacy of the blind man's perceptions never failed to amaze him. It was as if, though wounded, Shukri's senses gave him entry to another universe—a richer, more subtle one than that occupied by the sighted. Sometimes, at home, in the courtyard, Issa would tie his mother's black dusting rag around his eyes in order to wander, for a moment at least, in Shukri's onyx-black world of sound and touch.

Issa watched the silent nun drop the firewood at Shukri's feet. Then, in a move as reverent as it was swift, she laid her forehead against his sleeve and kissed it.

Issa heard Shukri say something sharp to her as he pulled his sleeve away—something about being a man like the others.

Then, wordlessly as she had come, the nun was gone.

"Baba, what was...?"

"Nothing, nothing, my son," Shukri mumbled, turning pale. "A little foolishness, that's all."

Wood chips had begun to sizzle in the belly of the stove.

"Tell me where we are," Issa asked, his eyes fixed once more on the fresco. "What convent is this?" He had never known such excitement. The ring had become a key to a whole new world.

The old man smiled. "Most of us call it The Chapel of the Terebinth," he said evenly. "After the painting."

(The intrigue in the word "us" did not escape the boy's notice.)

"But a few know it as the Church of St. Parakletos the Fatherless," Shukri continued. "Over there, under the marble slab at the foot of the altar—yes, his very bones," Shukri said, answering the boy's unasked question, "brought to Jerusalem centuries ago from the Syrian desert where he died."

Issa shuddered.

"Don't worry," the old man said quietly. "You've nothing to fear from him, from the Fatherless One. After all," Shukri added, his face suddenly grave, "he's one of us."

"Us...?" Issa could feel the word dropping inside him like a stone.

"Us, Issa," Shukri went on, his voice rising. "Like you and me, like the Messiah and the Virgin, like Joseph the Just and the Brethren of the Lord—the man who's buried here...is a Nazarene."

"Me...a Nazarene...." The boy's mind was a whirl of images: the ring, the icon of the oak tree, the grave—scrambled memories, the muddle of pain he heard buried in the word: Nazareth.

Shukri waited a long time before continuing. "You still think that the mystery is the *ring*, don't you?" the merchant asked in a voice that seemed somehow deeper and richer than before. "No, Issa, the mystery is something far more important than a ring. The mystery...is *you!*"

The old man pulled a folded piece of paper out of his coat pocket and waved it in the direction of the boy's voice.

Issa recognized it at once. It was the reply from his mother that Henry, half-drunk, had pressed into the merchant's hand earlier that night, on their way out of the cafe. The reply to Shukri's message.

The boy had asked to read it to him at the time. But the old man had stuffed the note into his pocket without a word.

Now his mother's words, dangling from Shukri's fingers, hung in the air between them like a door cut in the universe, like a space created for revelation.

Issa hadn't thought about the note a great deal. After all, what could the message say except to indicate whether or not Issa had permission to sleep at Shukri's house that night?

(And yet, what was it the brass man had hissed in his ear as he passed into the street, words half-heard at the time: "I *saw*

76

her..."?

Now he was afraid. The note—once uncomplicated, inno-cent—had become another border to cross in the journey of the ring.

The boy instinctively glanced over at the mysterious jewel, still on Shukri's hand. It was glowing like a coal in the firelight.

He opened the note. It was his mother's handwriting.

"Read it aloud, son," Shukri said from the shadows.

Just before his eyes focused on the words, Issa envisioned *her* face at the window of their house in the courtyard of the "No-Name" Saint. Her dark eyes lit by the kerosene lamp she always kept in the window sill, his mother, Myrna, waited. He could almost hear her voice behind the words as he read them, fogging up the glass with the circles her breath would have left there.

"You are right, dear friend," the message ran. "He is old enough to know. Tell him everything."

He was still trembling a little when the old man took his hand and shuffled across the room toward the sanctuary, toward the icon of the oak tree.

There, in its purple and green-gold shade, mats had been arranged on heavy rugs spread out on the sanctuary's age-buffed floor. The old merchant hung the large brass lamp on an iron hook and took his seat next to the still-shaken boy.

He invited Issa to rest his head against him.

"Now," Shukri said at last, with a sigh, "where were we...?"

TALE OF THE
OLIVE PRESS

Yitzhak pushed open the door with a palpable sense of relief. The long Passover ritual—the annual feast of his humiliation—was over.

His father had nodded to him that he might take his leave even before the family had finished singing the last of the Hallel Psalms. Usually, on such occasions, he was not dismissed before the men shuffled, pleasantly tired, into corners to murmur together texts from the commentaries about the Exodus from Egypt until, as the custom was, their eyes, perusing the holy text, could no longer distinguish between letters of the alphabet.

For Yitzhak, the dyslexia that overtook his uncles only on the threshold of sleep, was the misfortune of every hour. As the eldest son, he could hardly be passed over when ceremony demanded that the tale of the deliverance from Egypt be read. But, as the women said without malice, he had always been "slow," and the words would neither stay fixed in his memory nor free themselves without great effort from the humiliating net of his stutter.

It had always been like this. Children from neighboring villages on the Mount of Olives had always seen to it that he could taste the bitterness of his life, hurling stones at him whenever they spied the long-legged loping gait which was his trademark. Strong as a pack mule, he paid little attention to their physical threats.

But there were other harassments which were less easy to ignore. When village girls played the "Bridegroom Game," for example—an amusement in which the loser was obliged to find

Yitzhak and tell him to his face that she would marry him before she could rejoin the game.

Yitzhak, "the son of the promise," Yitzhak, "the one who laughs"—even his name was a cruel joke.

The orchard's moon-lit shadows seemed on this night to conspire in his humiliation, unrolling before his imagination a morass of indecipherable runes as he trudged down the rugged slope toward the olive presses, toward the place at the foot of the mountain locals call *Gat Shemanim*—Gethsemane. Dispossessed in a world where literacy was everything— gateway even, it seemed, to life with God—here, at least, the boy belonged, among the olive trees and the oil presses.

Even now, scurrying down the hill, Yitzhak found time to notice the placement of the smudge pots near the younger saplings, near the trees he called Boaz and Heber. The "Olive Man," in fact, had names for all his trees. They were his progeny and—what was even more important—they were his confidants. Yitzhak told his trees everything. Even at night, he could be seen walking alone in the groves, pouring out his vexations like water in their shade.

Bathed as they were this night in moonlight, their branches fanning like veils in the soft dry breeze, they were more than friends. They were an olive presser's bride.

Yitzhak reached for one of the goatskin lanterns which hung like gourds in the olive groves. No use stumbling about in the dark, he muttered. Had not the landlord, the Pharisee Nicodemus, ordered him to watch for the Master and his disciples?

(But why, he wondered, the order not to tell anyone, not to reveal the Master's whereabouts? Nicodemus had personally sworn him to silence in an embarrassed interview that afternoon. Well, the great ones have their mysteries, the boy concluded.)

The sound of the Hallels of a thousand Passovers ricocheted like rock-showers off the walls of Jerusalem's valleys. Yitzhak reasoned it would not be long now before the band of brothers would be seen hiking across the Kidron to seek shelter for the night, as arranged, in the olive harvesters' caves at the foot of the Mount of Olives.

How pleased they will be on such a cool night to see that fires have already been prepared in their caves, warming the damp enclosures for the vigil, he thought.

This was the young man's first chance to see the famous Galilean up close. When the Master had entered the Holy City with the pilgrims from Jericho, Yitzhak, unlike the rest of his brothers, had been "forbidden to waste his time" accompanying the Galilean to the Temple. (Those were his father's words.) In any case, Yitzhak had had the dunging of the trees to do.

Like everyone, he'd heard stories, of course, about *Yeshua ha-Notzri*, Jesus the Nazarene. Who in Jerusalem did not know about him? It was said one had but to kiss the fringes of his prayer shawl and...Yitzhak caught himself. The "slow" son of once-prosperous olive growers, reduced by the sins of fathers to the tending of the fertile orchards they once had owned: there were hardly merits enough there to warrant miracles.

Still, Yitzhak thought, it will be something to see him, just this once. His brothers, naturally, had been assigned to serve the needs of the distinguished guests all week, camping out as they did in their orchards. But his brothers were required at home tonight: to impress the relatives with their learning. The honor had, at last, fallen to him, by default.

Never mind, the boy mused. Did not the Torah say that Passover night was to be "a night of watching kept to the Lord by all the generations of Israel?" Well, tonight at least, Yitzhak thought with some satisfaction, I too will keep watch, serving the great Jesus of Nazareth.

Gray-blue smoke belched into the night air from the entrance of the low double-cave at the foot of the mountain. The fires reeked of damp weeds hastily gathered from the nearby dry wash. Shuffling could be heard, and the murmur of decidedly unfestive voices.

Yitzhak dropped the bundle of dry kindling he was carrying. The Master and his disciples were back! By the look of things, they'd arrived some time ago. Their seder must have ended early—very early indeed.

He felt a sudden knot in his stomach. He had not been there to so much as greet them or to make their fires or to fetch them water or to see if they had enough straw for their bedding or to bring more oil lamps for the hours of meditation ahead.

Jerusalem's humblest family prided itself on the care it lavished on pilgrims and strangers. Though he couldn't have anticipated the Master's early return, Yitzhak knew that his father would be furious if the rumor got around that they had mistreated, of all people, the Master of Galilee—and on Passover night.

He could hear his father's rebuke even now in his ears: "Do I not know you, Yitzhak? As sure as the night is dark, you wandered off to mend some broken branch or to warm some grove exposed to the winds or to whisper some secret to your beloved trees, forgetting all about your duties to our guests! Isn't it enough that you shame me in the streets of Jerusalem, must you embarrass me before..." he would stammer, unable to bring himself to finish the sentence.

A deep weariness, an exhaustion of the spirit, overtook the

young olive presser. What was to have been a signal honor on a day of liberation had been transformed in an instant into a long night's last humiliation.

Yitzhak set his jaw. Running away won't help, he told himself. Just get it over with.

It was a strange scene which confronted him at the cave. He had expected to find Jesus and his disciples singing and dancing as he had seen other rabbis do on the night of the feast. But it was silence instead which greeted him. He saw only a few dispirited men lounging around a wet smoking fire. Stranger still, most of the men were drowsing inside the cave, their faces covered with their rough-spun Galilean mantles.

No one even bothered to notice him as he removed the bramble from the fire pit, replacing it with chips of olive wood, or as he refreshed their animal skins with water from the well.

What could it mean, this unheard-of slumber? It was not yet even the middle of the night. Everyone knew that for men to fall asleep on Passover was to end the feast, to suspend the joys of redemption. His own brothers—by no means paragons of piety—had been known to stay awake over Passover tales until the crack of dawn.

And another thing: the Master. He was nowhere to be seen.

Suddenly a thought occurred to him, stinging the boy between the eyes like a fly: The Nazarene has gone to my father to lodge a complaint. The mix-up has spoiled their festivities, the festivities of eminent guests. And I, I alone, will be blamed!

Brambles dogged his tracks as he stumbled toward his father's house in the darkness. Gone was the beauty of the night, the fragrance of spring winds upon his face, the sweet fertility of the orchards which gave meaning and purpose to his life. For Yitzhak, the only reality now was remorse: remorse for the thousand tiny misadventures which plagued his days but, more terribly still, remorse for having ever been born at all.

Suddenly, the breath was knocked out of the husband-man. He had fallen over something in the shadows and found himself sprawled full-length on the ground, choking on dust.

He could hear himself breathing hard. He was trying to think. Every inch of the slope was a groove in his mind. Where exactly had he fallen, and over what? Perhaps a stray sheep or an unchained dog?

In any case, it was clear now where he'd fallen: Even in the dark he could make out the escarpment where the great olive presses were, where in the autumn they would press out the flesh of the hard bitter fruit until it yielded the golden oil that was the highlands' glory.

A long sigh arose, unbidden, from within him. Yitzhak shuddered. He'd never heard such a haunted sound before—not even in nightmares.

It was only when the groans continued that he realized that he was not their author, that he was not alone at the place of the pressing.

Yitzhak somehow knew not to call out, not to break the strange silence which had enveloped the clearing. As he strained forward on his knees to get a better look, he gradually made out the shape of a human figure, stretched out across the rock where they pressed the olives. The man was emitting sighs of such agony and innocence that, at first, Yitzhak had thought that a wounded animal had found its way there from the wastelands.

The voice was the sound of someone under unendurable

pressure, the voice of a man being broken.

Who could this be? Yitzhak, his mind strangely calm, perused the possibilities. Then, like the sudden dawning of the mind when a jumble of letters becomes a word, he realized who the man before him was.

"Yitzhak," the voice breathed after an interminable silence. "Watch with me."

TALE OF THE
MESSAGE

The news caught her completely off guard. "Arrested?" She could scarcely believe her ears. But, after all, it was not some Jerusalem gossip monger, but Artemius, a Temple guard, who had pulled Joanna aside with dark tidings as she ushered her guests into the windy Passover night.

"Arrested?" she hissed into his ear. "Are you sure?"

Her mind raced. "What could have gone wrong?" They had all suspected, all of them—the Twelve, the Master's family, the company of women, everyone—that the Caiaphas clique would make their move against the Master during the pilgrimage. That much was certain. But during the feast? On the night of the seder? Even a seasoned observer of Jerusalem intrigue like Joanna could not make sense of it. That Caiaphas, this year's High Priest, who for all his celebrated venality, was nothing if not shrewd, should have undertaken such a clumsy, even perilous, adventure....

Have our "Great Ones" forgotten what Roman soldiers do when confronted with angry Jewish mobs? The thought gripped her tightly.

And the Master? The possibility of him being in danger had never really occurred to her before. Oh, she had heard from Miriam of Migdal, the one from whom he had cast out seven demons, about what the Twelve called "The Dark Prophecies." But everyone said that it was difficult to know what to make of them—at least, that was what one told oneself.

No, their best intelligence on the Temple committees had specifically ruled out a Passover arrest. And the Master's whereabouts at every turn had been a closely guarded secret.

Only the Twelve had been appraised of virtually all his movements. They had been so very careful.

Questions scampered over one another in her mind like breeze-blown wool.

Where was Judas? Her key confidant among the disciples, keeper of the Master's purse, Judas should have come first thing to her. He didn't need to be told she had "influence." Her marriage to Chuza, the Herod family's steward, had seen to that. Even now, there was still time to prevent disaster, she thought, to pry the Master loose from Caiaphas' well-manicured paws.

One had only to ascertain his price. But she would need Judas' help: someone who could coordinate with the Twelve, someone who knew his way around the city's maze-like corridors of power. Any other time, if the Brotherhood had needed money, for example, Judas would have flown to her side on Mercury's heels. Where *was* the man?

Joanna scribbled a quick message and sent it with the guard into the Passover night. Unable to carry on under the circumstances with the after-dinner small talk upper-class Jerusalemites doted on these days, Joanna pleaded fatigue. Leaving the few remaining guests to the care of her husband, she pattered alone up narrow unlit stairs to the high rooftop terrace of Chuza's house, to think.

A scrawled parchment message, a tersely-worded plea sent in the dead of night, dry and brittle as Passover matzah— strange, thought Joanna, as she gazed into the brilliant desert starscape above her, a parchment note was what had brought the Master into her life in the first place.

Rich, powerful, equipped with a quick intelligence and a ready wit, Joanna had been so sure of herself in those days before the Master, so self-possessed.

That unforgettably serene summer on her uncle's oak-shaded villa above the shores of the Sea of Galilee had been shattered beyond repair by Menachem's sudden illness: Menachem, the youngest, the mischievous, the delight of Chuza's old age. It had descended upon them like one of the lake's famous storms—a child's morning chill out of nowhere turned into a raging fever by nightfall. Maidservants doing their best, Chuza moaning with anxiety.

They had, of course, heard stories about the local thaumaturge, Jesus the Nazarene, who was billeted with his followers in the nearby fishing village of Capernaum. They had caught a glimpse of him once near the fish market surrounded by the sick outside the door of the rude stone house of a local "big shot" named Shimon.

While allowing for the workings of God in principle, of course, Joanna had always disdained such things in practice. Neediness, however spiritual, always struck her as distasteful.

"No wonder the Romans consider us Jews superstitious," she had sniffed after viewing the chaotic spectacle at the disciple's door.

Days later, however, with her son's life slipping from her grasp, overwhelmed with a sense of her own powerlessness, she had bundled Chuza off to Capernaum in the dead of night with a desperate three word message to the Master: "Save my son!"

Long before her husband had had time to trundle the carriage back up the mountain with the wonder worker's reply, Menachem was sitting up, drinking bowl after bowl of broth and talking non-stop about the "man of light" who had awakened him.

Joanna had resolved that very night to become a follower

of Jesus, joining soon afterwards, with Miriam of Migdal, the Community of Women who supported the work of the disciples and saw to the Master's needs.

It had been her increasingly important role in organizing financial support for the Brothers which had brought Joanna into close association with the Master's treasurer, Judas of Iscariot.

Joanna strode to the edge of the great terrace with its incomparable view of the Temple.

The air, though touched with the chill of spring, was fragrant with the aroma of roasted meat, centerpiece of the city's myriad Passovers, coupled with the less seasonal, more unpleasant scent of the rivers of sacrificial blood shed on the Temple's altar every day. Her cynical uncle from Leontopolis always remarked during his annual visits to the city that, despite its beauty, "Jerusalem reeks like a village butcher's stall."

The indomitable Jerusalem matron surveyed the Temple precincts with a careful eye.

The huge alabaster mountain was silent tonight, like a dozing lion.

Joanna knew well, however, what stirred beneath its smooth marble hide. There, in the secret chambers where the priestly Sanhedrins met, Caiaphas toyed with the Master, probing the Galilean's words, looking for an opening, for unfortunate expressions and careless admissions.

Unhappily, Jesus had put himself within their grasp by his "prophetic violence" in the Temple, when he and his disciples dispersed the merchants and moneychangers from the Basilica.

Still, Joanna reasoned, Jesus had the wit of a fox. How

many times she had seen him silence the clever teams of lawyers sent by the powerful of Jerusalem to trip him up! They would have to prove some charge against him. And just where did Caiaphas and his lackeys hope to find sufficient corroborating witnesses on Passover night?

No, the Temple would have to disgorge its prey, Joanna reassured herself. Caiaphas might well wish himself rid of the troublesome Galilean. But on what grounds? Though a scoundrel, the High Priest was hardly an outlaw. The man was known to possess a fine legal, if not precisely ethical, sensibility. What capital charge could the man possibly impute to him? There had been grumblings among the elders about "that man's blasphemies." Would they try a blasphemy charge, perhaps? Joanna smiled. There's no more strictly applied principle in Jewish law, she told herself. No, they can't touch him on the basis of blasphemy.

Why, to do that, they'd have to get him to utter the forbidden Name, the Name the Holy One imparted to Moses on the Mountain, the Name forbidden to all except the High Priest, the great "I Am."

The knot in her stomach was slowly unwinding. No, they won't get away with it this time, the Annas and Caiaphas crowd, with their midnight hearings, their cunning back room maneuvers. Face to face with the unerring wit of innocence, they'll sputter and fizzle out like all the rest of them, the Master's official opponents.

What an issue we'll make of this little caprice, she cried, suddenly on fire. The matron could already visualize troops of shouting Jerusalemites denouncing the perverse "House of Boethus" in the streets, beneath their very windows. They've gone too far this time. We'll use the arrest to dislodge these well-fed, Roman-loving vultures from their perch. "We'll make you pay for this!" she found herself saying aloud, to Caiaphas, to the city, to the night.

Joanna was feeling better by the minute—focused, alert, sure of herself, aroused.

Yes, she cried to the stars, as Jesus saved my son Menachem from death, so I, Joanna, shall have the honor to rescue him from the clutches of the elders.

Had they not—Joanna and Jesus—a private joke between them about the text of her desperate message the night Jesus had raised her son from death? "Save my son," she had scribbled on the parchment. (The word "save" was a form of Jesus' own name "Savior.") "You see," he had smiled, giving the note back to her one day, "you really wrote not 'save my son,' but 'my son Jesus.'" Ever afterwards, they had shared this little intimacy between them.

Joanna sped around, resolute, her delicate porphyry robes flowing behind her in the wake of her determination as she reentered the house.

Chuza, as she had hoped, stood waiting for her in the vestibule. Good, she thought, he'll go to the Temple at once.

But her husband wore a strange, dispirited expression. Joanna could remember seeing that mask-like demeanor only once before, when Menachem lay panting for air on the mattress in Galilee.

"A message has come from Judas," he muttered.

It was not until hours later that Joanna came to understand the full import of the three-word message which unfolded itself before her eyes. Three words scrawled on the back of a parchment: "He is betrayed."

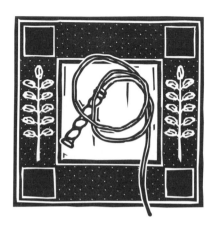

TALE OF THE
SCOURGE

T he appearance of Charon, nicknamed "the Scourge," was something of an event, even for the sort of Roman soldier who got farmed out to miserable imperial provinces like Judea—hard-bitten, "I've-seen-it-all-and-done-it-twice" sort of men.

They would have told you, if you had asked, that long before he was a sight to be reckoned with, Charon was a sound: the signature slither of his cobra-black whip across the smooth stone pavement, the lightning lick of its indeflectible bite.

No one ever thought of Charon without his whip. Over the decades, the thing had become like an appendage to his huge long-muscled arm; less like an extra member than a familiar spirit which he had managed to attach to himself. Even his voice—rarely heard—had, they said, developed a weird sibilating hiss.

"The procurator's 'Messiah Killer'," the captains would chortle as they waited for a flogging to begin, elbowing the words into the ribs of young skittish recruits. "Can't you hear him now in the tower, working his swift left hand," they would roar, "practicing on the bats?"

No doubt about it. Charon was the sort of man who invited nicknames and legends.

Given his status as Pilate's ace flogger, even his name seemed a macabre joke worthy of the gods: Charon, ferryman of dead souls over the river Acheron to the lower regions. A most efficient purveyor of souls, this Charon, one equipped with a particularly lacerating sense of humor. It was said by some that no sooner would he realize that a "patient" was about to die under the lash, than he would crouch on his haunches before him—this, to insure that he was the last thing the victim saw, even as life ebbed away.

Naturally, the chroniclers of the Guard had a field day with the man. He cut, after all, a rather colorful figure for himself in an otherwise dull-as-wax oriental court.

Few knew his history beyond the basics, however. Once a slave of the procurator's father, Caius, some service, deftly dispatched, had persuaded the old man to grant him his freedom. But Charon had opted to stay on as a paid employee of Pilate, the younger son. Why the man chose to serve Pilate particularly, no one knew for sure.

Fiercely loyal to his ambitious employer, he had functioned as a bodyguard until his duties were extended, the wags said, to performing the more unpleasant tasks of the young Pilate's mercurial rise. These were rumored to have included the gruesome murder of the future procurator's much-loved elder brother, Demetrius. But that was not established. No one had been able to lay that wreath on Pilate's door. And Charon, they said, had grieved bitterly at the funeral, mourning Demetrius like a son.

Upon arrival in Judea, Pilate, bodyguarded now by crack troops, had lost no time finding suitable work for his Egyptian daemon. Eager to avoid the costly bloodbaths of his predecessor Varus and to curry favor with Rome, Pilate sought to crush Jewish nationalist hopes even before they had an opportunity to adorn themselves with martyrs.

Enter Charon, wielder of the scourge extraordinaire.

"I will let all Jerusalem see how I shall crush the life out of these rebels," Pilate had let slip to Herod Antipas, tetrarch of Galilee, over supper (he had crushed a Jericho grape between his fingers for effect), "long before they ever reach the 'glory' of the cross."

And so it was not long before Pilate's shadowy aide had acquired yet another nickname. As he passed in his litter in the streets, Jerusalem's children called him *Ha Magraysah*—"Crusher of Bones."

Charon's entrance into the Lithostrotos was as simple as it was sudden.

The cohort, 600 strong, had grown restless under the canopy of the cool Jerusalem night, with its pitiless spring joint-rusting damps. They had played a form of the old Basileus game with the prisoner. As usual in these cases, he had been paraded around in the chlamus, the deep red military cloak, to the typical obscene lyrics; the special treat for Jewish rebels—the circlet of thorns, made up to look like the radiant crown of Tiberius Caesar—had been rammed onto his brow.

But the soldiers, uncharacteristically subdued for such a proceeding, had soon reformed in ranks, awaiting the "Scourge." The bone-numbing gusts which had begun whipping down the valleys from the highlands had robbed them, for the moment at least, of their enthusiasm for these rites of humiliation.

And then there was the prisoner himself. Something about the impenetrable quality of his silence—something indefinable, but palpable nonetheless—had unnerved the men. In the night which swirled about the mock-King, the cohort was like a snowbound unit going through the motions of a battle which the muscles of its engines could not execute.

And then, out of nowhere, there was the sound, indistinct at first, like the distant shuffling of feet or the dragging of a sack of flour, but then suddenly sharp as the crack of gladiators' bones, like the voice of a whip wide as a cobra. Without a word, light on his feet for so large a man, Charon strode like a shadow across the slick, smooth pavement.

People, on seeing the most feared man in Jerusalem for the first time, invariably remarked about the torturer's face. Suspended above an immense breadth of shoulder, Charon's features were oddly delicate, beautiful even. Under the crown of close-cropped, graying hair shone the great eyes of an impassive boy, unblinking, fixed on something in the far distance, something perhaps not even on a map. Under the circumstances, the bizarre, unexpected innocence on the face of the "Crusher of Bones" was more terrifying than if the man had been a cyclops.

The soldiers stood at attention as Charon approached to get a better look at his prey, standing at the far corner of the Lithostrotos, draped absurdly in the trappings of a cruel charade, the rising wind whipping the royal mantle about him like giant wings.

Charon suddenly stopped in his tracks, as if by the word of an unseen command. His face, still impassive, unreadable, locked on the eyes of his prisoner.

"Who are you?" the deep voice of the torturer growled.

The cohort relaxed a little, laughing nervously, ready for the vintage mind-games which were Charon's cruel specialty.

But instead, the torturer let the great whip slip from his grasp like an amputated limb, its silver griffin's knob clanging in the pavement grooves.

"What?" he shouted. "You come to mock me?"

He rushed upon the prisoner like a wrestler, wrenching the man's face toward his—gaze against gaze—his eyes contorted with rage.

Finally, his head shaking with confusion, he reclaimed his whip with a swift sure motion and hissed: "Strip him! The boatman's got work to do!"

The "Bone Crusher" raised his arm for one last stroke, one last lash in the direction of the silent prisoner who was bleating for breath in the misting darkness.

But the shoulders of Pilate's henchman would have no more of it. The whip rose in the air like a sizzling ribbon and fell to the pavement, crumpling next to its owner on the hard gleaming stone.

The cohort had been dismissed long ago to its harvest of bad dreams. Only Longinus, the centurion, lingered at the far end of the Lithostrotos, in case the prisoner should die, in case an official's stamp should be required on the final papers.

Charon was a mass of quivering muscle. He had never beat anyone like that before—never.

Even the soldiers had been unable to watch the savage pummeling. The men had come to watch a public degradation, full of the Egyptian's trademark wit, the cunning of the mighty whip. They had come to watch an arrogant provincial rebel grovel before his masters.

Instead, they had witnessed a snorting butcher whack away for what seemed like hours at a bleeding carcass—silent, as it turned out, to the end.

The Egyptian, still twisted in a heap, began muttering to himself. "Why does he not die—the long dead Demetrius?" Each word dropped like a stone into the pool of the night.

"And why," he asked, crouching toward the feet of his silent, bleeding captive, "do I find his face, the face of the one man who loved me, alive again—in yours?"

Pilate's master torturer leaned his long sweating torso against the white marble post where the body of Jesus still hung, shaking in shock against the chains.

98

TALE OF THE
OAK TREE

Wood chips flew like diving sparrows across the narrow confines of the contractor's stall: a flock of birds caught in a dust storm.

Normally, the whoosh of Shimon's plane smoothing the surface of an oak log would have drawn a few admiring Jerusalemites to crowd the low entrance of his rough-plastered workshop in the "Cheesemongers" valley.

"He carves wood with as pure a knife as the ritual butcher's," the passersby would nod to each other, watching the shape of a plow or yoke emerge from the womb of branchwood in a matter of minutes.

But today Jerusalem's most reliable "jack-of-all-trades" worked alone, unattended, racing against time and detection.

It wasn't bad enough that Shimon was betraying his God by working on Passover. (His wife had told the neighbors that he was paying a Passover visit to a house in the northern suburbs.) He had also managed to add betrayal of his people to the misdeeds of this cool sunny morning after the seder. (Who would make his excuses for that, he wondered.) Shimon, Jerusalem's most skillful *tekton*, Shimon "the Builder," was working for the Romans.

The craftsman shivered. His doorway sealed with a thick leather curtain, the darkness penetrated by a few smoking lamps, he could not so much as think of lighting even the smallest fire to relieve the cold. Situated in the low valley which divided the Holy City in two, even a wisp of smoke from the clay oven at the back of the shop would attract attention.

"Jews don't light new fires on their feasts," Shimon had explained to the Roman officer who sat on the stool behind him, rubbing his hands. "Well then, hurry up, man," the Roman had barked.

"Just as well," Shimon muttered bitterly, biting once more into the oakflesh with his bronze-tipped plane. But his well-honed skills seemed to have deserted him. The wood resisted his attempts to shape it into the long, heavy *patibulum*, the crossbar, upon which the pagans hung their Jews.

It didn't require great intelligence to figure out why the Roman military engineers nearly always demanded the hard, tough wood of the oak for their crucifixions. While olive wood was far more plentiful, it was soft and unreliable. Crucified men left alone to die on isolated roads had been known to wriggle free of its grasp. Oakwood, on the other hand, the tree of endurance and triumph, could bear great weight without splitting. Like the ash, the oak was said by the ancients to be so bold as to court lightning.

But Shimon, who was something of an expert in the lore of trees, knew that the pagans had more in mind in their selection of woods than merely practical considerations. He might be a Palestinian Jew, but did the Romans really imagine that craftsmen living at such a crux of trade routes would not be aware that the oak tree was sacred to Jupiter Olympus, the chief Roman deity?

Had not their poet Virgil once sung the praises of the pistachio oak, the tree whose roots extend as far underground as its branches rise in the air? Did their wise men not consider the oak an emblem of the god whose rule extends from the heavens to the underworld?

Behind all the political issues of the Roman occupation of

Judea, even the poorest of Israelites knew that a great spiritual conflict raged: a dark battle of Powers. Was it mere coincidence that the idol-worshipers insisted on humiliating the devotees of the One True God on wood holy to their own accursed Zeus?

But Shimon knew other traditions about the oak, traditions taught to him when he was an apprentice contractor in Galilee, when he had been an apprentice to a Nazarene builder named Joseph in the years shortly after Varus, the "Roman Butcher," had crucified thousands there on the northern roadways.

Besides being an expert builder, Yosef ben Yakov had been a master of the mysterious properties of plants and trees. There simply wasn't a feature of the Nazareth Mountains the man didn't know: the names and medicinal uses of its wildflowers, the whereabouts of hidden springs, the precise few days after the latter rains when the black crocus would bloom like dried blood on Gilboa, the day of the midsummer flowering of the terebinth.

"Have you not read the writings of Jesus ben Sirach?" Joseph quizzed him soon after the apprentice had begun working for him. "There it's said that the divine Wisdom itself dances on our hills and in our fields."

I grew tall like a cedar in Lebanon,

Joseph chanted in his mellifluous voice,

> *and like a cypress on the heights of Hermon.*
> *I grew tall like a palm tree in Engedi,*
> *and like rosebushes in Jericho;*
> *like a fair olive tree in the field,*
> *and like a plane tree beside water....*

Like cassia and camel's thorn
I gave forth perfume,
and like choice myrrh
I spread my fragrance...,
Like a terebinth I spread out my branches,
and my branches are glorious and graceful.
Like the vine I bud forth delights,
and my blossoms become glorious and abundant fruit.

Once resting together with Joseph and his young son Jesus in the summer shade of a great terebinth above Nazareth, the older man had spoken at length about the tree. Shimon had never been able to forget his words.

The oak and the terebinth, he had related, are unique among living things in that they bear the name of God. In fact, said Joseph, they are related in other ways as well. "The terebinth is the spirit of the oak," he said mysteriously.

Because the terebinth is the "God-tree," it was natural that Joshua should have sealed the covenant under its branches at Shechem and that David should have proved victorious over Goliath in the Valley of Terebinths.

"Nevertheless," he said, "the greatest deeds done in the shade of the terebinth are yet to come."

"How can there be greater deeds than these?" Shimon had asked him.

"When our Father, Abraham, stopped at Hebron under the great tree of Mamre," the old man went on, "it was because the Patriarch had been told that the grove was the site of the creation of Adam, the first man, and the Mamre terebinth, the tree of the knowledge of Good and Evil, beneath whose shade he had been tempted."

"One day," said Joseph, while showing his boy how to

open an acorn with one hand, "another Adam will do battle under a terebinth tree. This new Adam will make a door into the reign of God."

"A door?" the boy had asked.

"Of course," his father had smiled. "Do we not use only the sturdy oakwood for the framing of our doorways? Oak alone of the woods can bear the weight of stone. Well, the oak is the door-tree. In its shade, by sin, the first Adam sealed our passage. But another one," he said as he cracked the sweet meat of an acorn into his son's hand, "will tear it open again."

The Roman officer ran his hand over the stone-hard skin of the finished crossbar. He lifted the end of the *patibulum* to test its weight.

"You were right to obey orders," the officer said as the *tekton* oiled his tools. "Longinus will see to it that you won't go unrewarded."

"I don't want his money," Shimon mumbled into the wall.

"Well, in any case," the officer gazed at him, "you had no choice. You're the only really competent carpenter in Jerusalem."

Feeling the cowardice wrenching his bowels like spoiled meat, Shimon said quietly, "And if I'd refused?"

"Egypt," the Roman snapped, "exile," as he thumped the wood for weak spots. "Tomorrow would have found you and your family on the road to Alexandria. Your house, your shop, your tools—shall we say 'bequeathed' to more cooperative, if less talented, craftsmen."

"May I ask you something...?" Shimon said after a long pause, barely getting the words out of a dry, tightening throat. The master builder knew well for whom the crossbar had been fashioned, which young body would have the life drained out of it, perched on its two dark wings. He had seen the name written in the rivers of woodgrain he had traversed with his agile plane. He had felt the man's hand, even from prison, restraining the flight of his double-winged tool.

"Well?" the Roman said, distracted with the arrival of two recruits sent to convey the crossbeam to the Praetorium.

"The man who will be crucified—may I know his name?" Shimon wanted to be sure. After all, he knew Barabbas' family personally.

"Against regulations, I'm afraid. But," he said with a smile of barely disguised contempt, "you'll hardly be in the mood to run right out and raise a mob against us, right?"

The words hit like a blow.

"After all, it's *your* handiwork," the Roman sniffed, rubbing the crossbar one last time. "Don't tell Longinus I told you," he threatened as he pulled open the workshop's leather curtain, "but it's that Galilean, Jesus of Nazareth, the one the governor calls 'King of the Jews.'"

At the mention of that name, before he even had time to assimilate what he'd been told, Shimon's nostrils flooded with the smells of a summer afternoon in Galilee, long, long ago, when, in the shadow of the great terebinth tree, a door had opened to the sky.

TALE OF THE
MAGIC JEWEL

The Lady Mosella turned to face the first hint of sea breeze in the Jerusalem air. Right on schedule, she thought as she continued to examine the large blue-green emerald on her fingertips in the golden afternoon light.

Better than a sundial, the wonderful Mediterranean breezes which wended their way through the city this same time each afternoon, towards the end of the siesta, unwinding the bitter coils of temper which were Jerusalem's trademark, freshening the air, bridging, if only for a moment, the city's oriental isolation with the fragrance of a Roman and imperial sea.

These "westerlies" always reminded the young matron of the world of Caesarea, her world. *Caesarea Maritima*—Caesar's city by the Sea—sometimes she really thought that she loved it more than Rome. Modern, cultured, sleek, teeming with young people and new ideas, Palestine's provincial capital, headquarters of the Roman administration of the country—Caesarea was, as her husband once joked at a dinner party, a breathtaking white lion licking its paws in a jungle clearing.

The jungle, that was Jerusalem.

How Mosella hated these oriental cities—Alexandria, Antioch, Ptolemais, Berytus—to which they'd been assigned. Jerusalem, worst of all. Oh, they all sported a veneer of Roman culture and civilization. But she could feel herself overwhelmed in their close, rank streets by older, darker forces which lay just beneath the surface civility, awaiting their day.

"We're not really in control here, you know," Mosella had suggested to Pontius Pilate, her husband, during last year's

Passover trek to Jerusalem. "They let us think we are," she said darkly.

Pilate's surprise had not escaped her. She spoke little and never on the subject of politics. Mosella was, after all, barely out of her teens. And she knew how her spouse disapproved of wives who sought to become their husbands' professional colleagues. "It's an entirely un-Roman attitude," he would say.

Nevertheless, she'd felt compelled to warn him. He was much too sure of himself, much too taken with his own cleverness.

On that occasion, Pilate contented himself with pinching her cheek: "Well," he quipped, "I've got a new vice-procurator, it seems."

The jewel glinted in her hand like the surface of a green sea, lit from below. Her grandfather, the Roman general Caius Vitellius, had given her the gem when she had still been a child. "It goes with the name," he had told her, "Mosella, green as the river I crossed with Julius Caesar's legions in the Belgian Gaul so many years ago."

When she had grown older, he regaled her on her name-day with tales about the gem.

Tossing the emerald gently, like a cooling ember, in the palm of his soldier's hand, Vitellius informed his favorite granddaughter that the stone had once been an amulet belonging to a powerful Gallic chieftain captured by the Romans. He had won it during the casting of lots for the pagan's valuables, just before the man was beheaded.

The barbarian had called it "the pardoning stone," he told her. When rolled at the feet of a man condemned to death, the prisoner had to be freed instantly.

"Is it magic, Grandfather?" she had asked him time and time again.

But all the old general would say was that he had reason to believe that the jewel possessed "certain [unspecified] powers." He would go on to quote "our Roman authors" on the subject, pointing out that the emerald was considered a "harbinger of truth" and that among its faculties was said to be the "quickening of prophecy."

When Mosella would plead for an explanation, Vitellius would answer only that "the ancients say you can see things in it." More he wouldn't say, no matter how many times she implored him.

Nevertheless, the old general routinely warned her to keep the jewel from "curious eyes."

The Lady Mosella had kept her word. Even people in her own household were largely unaware that she possessed such a trophy.

But Mosella, in the privacy of her chambers, often consulted the charm when her sleep was "disturbed." Caught perhaps in this brilliant bubble of color, some shape, some suggestion of a word written in light, could provide a clue to the meaning of the strange things she so often glimpsed in dreams.

Last night, when the wind was up and she had seen *that* face, his face, a Jew's face, spattered with blood, an imperial corona radiating from his brow.... And then, when she had seen the man himself—in a chance passing by an open door— that man (she was sure of it), in a private audience with her husband that morning, bathed in sunlight in the Hall of Judgment....

But the emerald kept its secrets to itself. No matter how many times she held it to the light, the only magic it offered on this spring afternoon was its own sea-green beauty.

The Procurator of Judea took his time answering his

wife's summons. He had managed three criminal cases and the review of a legal brief before lunch. And there was still more to do before the Jewish Levites blasted their silver trumpets from the Temple Mount, announcing the end of another vexing day in the life of a provincial Roman officer.

Mosella could see at once that her husband was in rare form when he finally sauntered into her chambers above the courtyard.

"Well, my dear," he said, taking a green apple from a marble bowl, "it's been a 'red-letter' day for the governor of Judea, I'd say. I've got Caiaphas and the Jerusalem notables just where I want them," he sniffed. "And all because of that man, the Nazarene prophet they hauled in this morning." He took a bite out of his apple. "Really, I ought to give the man some sort of reward. Even Herod Antipas, the Tetrarch, is foaming at the mouth. It's just too delicious."

He went on to recount how he had managed to play off "the Nazarene" against the elders, a move which was sure to win points with "the mob," let alone Rome. "And the fellow's 'royal bearing' has the Herods quaking in their boots that he's some sort of secret long-lost claimant to the throne. What'll the dampening of that fire be worth in gold talents, I wonder?

"The greatest thing," he told his wife, "is that I have complete freedom of action. If I help the notables get rid of their 'upstart,' they'll be in my debt for years to come. I'll have finally succeeded putting Jerusalem's 'high and mighty' in their place. And if I rescue their 'king,' why, I'll practically be a nationalist hero," he crowed. "I really didn't imagine such sophisticated political entertainment would be available out here in the provinces. It almost—I said *almost*," he added, looking for the first time in his wife's direction, "makes one wish to spend more than one or two weeks a year in this

110

benighted city."

"Now," he said, addressing his wife, "what was it that was so urgent, my Lady? Why, you're trembling, Mosella! What has happened?" asked Pilate, going to his wife, trying to impose a "concerned husband" look on his features.

Mosella swallowed hard several times before stammering in a low voice, "Have nothing to do with this man, Pilate." The emerald dug into her palm as she closed her fist upon it. "I have had a dream."

Pilate stood silently for some minutes before responding. The situation needed careful handling. Irritation was rising in his throat. This marked the second time in as many trips to Jerusalem that his young unworldly wife had seen fit to interfere in his affairs. He had married the Lady Mosella precisely because she'd been educated as a virgin of Cybelle. This had augured a quiet domestic life with a wife who would make minimal demands, firmly ensconced in her domestic routines, leaving a man largely free to come and go as he pleased.

And yet, he dare not make her unhappy. The Lady Mosella's family had the most powerful connections in Rome. It would not do to offend her.

"My dear, is that all?" Pilate ventured at last. "Dreams and oracles: They're notoriously capricious, are they not?"

"Say what you like, Pilate, but have nothing to do with his condemnation," she stammered again. "I saw Augustus himself...worshiping his wounds."

"All right, my dear, all right," Pilate grimaced, turning from her with a sharp movement. He had come to a firm decision: Mosella would never accompany him to Jerusalem again.

(Of course, that last little obscenity, Pilate reasoned—the

comment about Augustus worshiping a Jew—that might bear remembering. Should he need grounds one day for "distancing" himself from her....)

As he sped out of the chamber, Mosella opened her clenched fists in relief. The emerald pattered over the stone floor in front of her. For the first time, she noticed the wedge-shaped wound it had left in her clear white palm.

TALE OF THE
DICE

W here had all the sunlight gone? Longinus, the centurion, wondered as he fastened the light military cloak about his shoulders. He would have equipped himself with a wool mantle for the day's imperial errand had he foreseen that a mid-morning squall was brewing.

From the height of the old quarry beyond the Genath Gate, Longinus watched the dark clouds spread like a veil over the city. The "westerlies" were inexplicably early, he noted, bringing with them not fragrant Mediterranean breezes, but an alpine chill out of nowhere which cut right through clothing.

Cursing, the centurion ordered his men to light a fire and watched as the skyscape grew more ominous still. Swallow swarms whirred madly about as fast-moving winds overhead threw the city's pestilential dust into the air like a crazed mourner.

In the distance, a bizarre counterpoint of light and shadow played itself out over the contours of the desert as sunlight and shreds of blue sky were rent by shafts of heat lightning only to be smothered in sheets of sludge-black rain.

While his men exchanged quizzical glances and barked orders at the crowds to reassure themselves, Longinus stood still, a hand lightly resting on the hilt of his sword, his eyes fixed on the vista before him. He, for one, did not need to consult the manuals for an explanation of these omens. He knew well for whom the heavens performed.

The centurion had not been able to look the prisoner in the face, not once, distracting himself instead with a mime of

114

restless activity, a burlesque of power. But he could feel the fix of gray eyes upon the nape of his neck. He could hear the halting recitation of the prisoner's prayer buzz in his ear:

> *"Eli, Eli, lama sabachtani,*
> *rahoq mishuati dibrei sha'agati...."*

> "My God, my God, for what purpose
> have you forsaken me
> or cast yourself far from
> the words of my cry?"

> *"Va'atah kadosh*
> *yoshayv tiheelot Yisrael...."*

> "And yet you are holy,
> still enthroned upon the songs of Israel,
> praising your mighty deeds."

"You understand what he's saying, sir?" one of the soldiers, gazing at the crucified one, asked. "Some sort of Jewish magic?"

Longinus edged forward slightly to indicate to a clot of the man's relatives that they might draw nearer to the condemned.

He was feeling increasingly ill. Why had Pilate insisted that he alone stage manage this particular execution? How he had tried to get the assignment palmed off on another officer when he found out that the one condemned to death was not Barabbas. Why had Pilate insisted? Any Jewish rebel but this one!

"No, not magic, sergeant," he sighed, addressing the man behind him. "It's the traditional prayer of a man unjustly condemned, awaiting deliverance from the gods."

"Fat chance," the soldier spat before joining his companions at the fire.

But Longinus grew more anxious by the minute. After all, he had read the wrenching Psalm as a boy. Did not its superscription read: "To Him who grants victory"? He looked up to see clouds roiling in the heavens like an angry sea.

"By the gods! What I wouldn't give to get this over with!" Longinus muttered, bundling his cloak about him.

"Sir! Sir!" the men shouted at him from the fireside. The centurion managed a wan smile as he pulled out the requisite three dice from the leather pouch hanging at his side.

"Ah, yes. The final indignity," he said as he strode toward them.

Dice: It was the first clue the soldiers of the garrison in Caesarea had had that Longinus, Pilate's new legal adviser on military affairs, was not going to be the usual sort of fast-talking martinet Rome invariably assigned to provincial units. Even during the centurion's first review of his troops, the men had not failed to notice the telltale ivory "bone" he tossed in his hand.

Well, the men nodded to each other. Things were looking up. For it was clear as a Mediterranean noon that the centurion Longinus was a gambler.

Armed with a handful of *tesserae luxoriae*, the Greek six-sided dice, the centurion lost no time in proving them right. Within months, there was hardly a senior officer in the battalion who had not seen at least several weeks' wages spirited away by Longinus' lightning roll in the "all or nothing" games which were his specialty.

"Three sixes or three aces"—the centurion's invariable invitation to the contest of "total chance"—had practically become the Caesarean guard's secret motto, along with Longinus' cheerful "The goddess still is faithful," as he tabulat-

116

ed his usually generous winnings.

Naturally, this good-humored fleecing of their commanders soon made the centurion the most popular man in the Guard, earning him the barracks moniker *Filius Fortuna*—"Fortune's Boy."

Even Pilate, who, like many conservative Romans, disapproved of gambling on principle, made jokes about it. When the procurator's military adviser could not be quickly located, Pilate would smile and say, "Oh, I see. You mean Longinus is at his 'devotions'?"

(Actually, Pilate merely thought the practice "lower class" and worried lest Longinus' aptitudes should create division in his senior staff.)

"No," Pilate had confided once to the Syrian legate, who had inquired about the rumors he'd heard, "the man gambles with such"—he searched the air for a word—"abandon, as if he doesn't care in the least about winning. That, naturally, is what makes it more or less tolerable, don't you think? If the man were serious about it, that would be an altogether different matter."

But Longinus *was* serious about his little dance with the fickle goddess Fortuna. That is, ever since his grandfather's bequest had made him independent of his father, and of his father's scruples.

"Say what you will, there aren't many Romans like my father," Longinus told his companions—adding, "May the gods be praised" to himself. At least grandfather betrayed himself for money, Longinus reasoned. My esteemed father, a Roman officer and a gentleman, has seen fit to align himself with the Jewish "reactionaries" out of love.

Love for the one tribe on the face of the earth which has stood squarely in the face of progress? Time and again, Longinus had hurled these words in his father's face. These people with their One True God: as if all the gods were not just *names*—different names for the same thing. This, Longinus had never been able to fathom.

Actually, that was not quite true. There had been a time—after his sickness—when, on the brink of manhood, he had managed to learn a smattering of Hebrew and had accompanied his father to the synagogue. It was after one of their wonder workers, the Nazarene, Jesus, had cured him of the fever.

But had his father really expected him to follow in his footsteps after that? To forever be a stranger in someone else's house? To live as half a Roman in a Roman's world? And for what recompense? To be granted the immeasurable favor of being called a "proselyte," a "convert" by *them* for the rest of one's days?

"Even you, with all your devotion, haven't managed to submit to their barbaric rite—to circumcision—now, have you?" Longinus had once shouted at him, a misstep for which he had later apologized. After all, it wasn't a very "Roman" thing to do—to lose one's temper at a parent.

In any case, the die had been cast when Longinus had been sent to Caesarea. A morning in the gymnasium had cured him forever of any attachment to Israel, or to Israel's forbidding deity. He had been set right by the whispers of the other youths, as though he had some secret disease, by the boys who surrounded him, demanding to know if he had been "mutilated," if the blade of circumcision had ever touched him!

No, the clean sea air, the manly splendor of Roman games, the easy tolerance of pagan society: The impact of his father's world seemed to fade overnight. "I am a child of the fates now," he had informed him.

118

They tossed the dice, one after the other, on the magician's seamless robe. "Magician"—the soldiers had picked that epithet up from the priestly claque sent to the site to protest Pilate's bold *capitulus*: *Hic est Iesus Nazareus Rex Iudeorum*—"This is Jesus the Nazarene, King of the Jews."

Longinus at first played absently, aware only of the tension in the air, the strange silence which hung over the darkened city, the dove-like cries of the mourning women.

Uneasiness was washing over him in waves. Always before, he'd managed to distance himself from the dark face of what Romans had to do to keep control of Judea. A step removed—that was Longinus: adviser on military cost-cutting, a bureaucrat of occupation, a signature on death warrants. Always before, Longinus, the skeptical bystander of the war Rome waged against the Jews.

But the centurion could not now avoid the sputter of heavy breathing at his back, the terrible gaze of innocence which confronted him on the cross.

Here before him were not abstract notions of progress and the good life—the facile bathhouse talk of Caesarea—but the magic of death and power, the threat of crimes that cry to heaven.

It was his turn at the dice.

As he knelt down on his haunches for the throw, he realized that, for the first time in his gambling career, he wanted something. He wanted the "magician's" robe.

Why exactly he couldn't have said. Perhaps to return it to the man's family, to save at least that shred of clothing from dishonor. Perhaps to use it as a bargaining chip: to lessen a growing sense of implication in a wrong which had, quite noticeably, attracted the attention of the gods.

"Three sixes or three aces," he declared with his trademark

laugh, "all or nothing," as he rolled the ivory tessera onto the wind-stirred surface of the robe.

He could see himself bundling the garment into his gear. He could see himself placing the dead man's robe, neatly folded over, into the hands of his father, turning aside questions, avoiding the otherwise inevitable explanations, easing the conscience that was already gnawing at his insides like a ferret.

He reached for the dark red peasant's cloak.

"But you've lost, sir," a soldier exclaimed. "Didn't you see?" All the men were looking at him. "The cloak belongs to Rufus."

TALE OF THE
NARD

B *aruch dayyin ha-emet*: "Blessed be the true judge." They had been Joseph's first words on hearing the news that Jesus of Nazareth was dead.

Joseph's eyes, their lights gone out as he uttered the prayer, declared the quiet end of hope, the sentence breathed more than spoken, as a husband might when forced to tell his wife that a particularly beloved child had died. "We were not wrong to have believed, my dear," the councilman said, trying to comfort her, but announcing instead the death of his own faith. Then he had performed the ritual of the rending of garments, ripping his sleeve from end to end.

But for Miriam ha-Migdali, the woman his disciples called "the Magdalene," as she hiked between the rugged scrub-brushed boulders toward the tomb, the words seemed less a gesture of pious resignation than a portent. "Blessed be the true judge"—the words were like a script written on the clear night sky, a promise yet unborn.

Where had she found the courage to say to the old man before he went to beg the body from Pilate: "Men have judged, eminence, men have killed; not God"?

But the Master had always called the former prostitute his "prophetess." In her former occupation, she had been an artful interpreter of an admirer's merest glance; now, in her repentance, she had become, he said, the most intuitive of his followers.

"Do you not understand?" he asked his disciples. "There is sacred fire concealed in the darkness of every sin. Repentance liberates the fire."

The Master had called her "prophetess" one final time when she had welcomed him to the Holy City by anointing his five senses with the last jar of the precious ointments which had once been the tools of her trade.

"She has done this to prepare me for my burial," he had remarked to a highly discomfited group of disciples on that occasion. The smell of the nard lingered still on her long delicate fingers.

Though outwardly composed, she found herself trembling with a strange inner excitement. Anxiety, grief, anger, hurt, tenderness, fury—all these had seethed inside of her as she had watched him die. But as she made her way down sheep paths in the neck of sunken land along the walls, the Magdalene felt like a woman awaiting the imminent return of her lover.

> *Upon my bed at night*
> *I sought him whom my soul loves;*
> *I sought him, but I found him not,*

she sang to herself,

> *I will rise now and go about the city....*

Her cantillation bounced over the terrain like the distant bells of a bedouin herd. This is hardly the night to be singing out loud beneath the walls of Jerusalem, she thought, catching herself, pulling her long black mantle over the lower part of her face. Roman soldiers were watching the approaches to the city like hawks. Brigands from the southern wadis had been spotted earlier that evening by townspeople on the Hebron road, attracted by the large numbers of Jerusalemites whom the afternoon temblors had sent scurrying out of the city.

The earth still quivered from time to time like a child who refuses to be consoled.

The Magdalene had heard rumors that other ominous signs had appeared in the Temple that day: the great door to the *Hechal*, the Holy Place, had opened by itself, it was said. More disturbing still, aftershocks had sent slabs of masonry from the Temple's southeast corner tumbling into the Kidron Valley. And a black raven had careened into the alabaster face of the Treasury, spattering it with blood.

The spring moon glistened in the waters of the great reservoir west of Jerusalem as the Magdalene concealed her journey in the pine groves that ringed it. Above her, the white towers of the Holy City's Western Gate buzzed with activity. Watchmen scoured the landscape from the walls of Herod's marble palace. They were looking, she suspected, not merely for highwaymen, but also for signs of movement at her place of destination, the craggy limestone rise just outside the Genath Gate where the Master's body lay.

> *The watchmen found me*
> *as they went about in the city....*

The music again stole into her head.

> *Have you seen him whom my heart loves?*

How he had loved to hear her sing the Song of Solomon when the Company of Women brought fresh food and supplies to the Brothers!

The Master would put up his hand to silence the disciples while the women sang at their chores. "Listen, brothers, and learn from them," he would say. "The Magdalene has taught them her [love] songs."

The Master would smile as he watched the disciples squirm. Though the chief aide of the Master's own mother, *Miriam ha-Migdali* had always made the Twelve noticeably uncomfortable. They doubtless would have preferred Joanna, the steward's wife, or some other "notable" to organize their support. Judas, for one, was quite vocal about "avoiding unnecessary scandal" by giving the former "Phoenician actress" so public a role in the Ministry.

But the Master was adamant. "Because of her great love, much has been forgiven her. The greatest enemy to the Work of God is not an evil reputation"—at this, the Master always smiled—"but an evil heart. What does a man gain by having a great and pious name if, all the while, his soul is small? That is the deep meaning of the Magdalene's repentance." At this, he would tap the cheek of the youngest, John, whose laughter was his special delight.

The Magdalene surveyed the terrain carefully before she left the protection of the glen to set out on the last leg of her journey. The afternoon squall had shattered several of the larger pines, filling the copse with the sweet smell of resins, like the spices Nicodemus had brought in preparation for the Master's burial.

> *I arose to open to my beloved,*
> *and my hands dripped with myrrh,*
> *my fingers with liquid myrrh...,*

the fragrances whispered, reminding her of the desolation she had witnessed only hours before.

The women had waited at a distance as John—"the disciple whom Jesus loved"—and the two Pharisees, Nicodemus and Joseph, had entered the newly-quarried tomb beside the Genath to perform the Master's *tohorah*, washing the blood off his wounds with lukewarm water, trimming his nails and combing his hair for the day of judgment, when the dead will rise again.

She could smell then, even at such a distance, the scent of

the Eaglewood—the aloes—which graced the clean linen shroud in which they laid him.

> *Your robes are all fragrant with myrrh,*
> *with aloes and cassia...,*

the verses swam in her mind.

Miriam climbed to the top of the ridge called the Akra. Even in the darkness she could tell that the spikes of crucifixion were still in place on the little nub of quarried stone where they had slain him. The city wall met her gaze before she hazarded a look into the narrow ravine where plentiful caves had suggested tombs for the Jerusalem aristocracy.

There in the darkness, swallowed in stone, lay the body of all her hopes—indeed, as far as she could tell, the hopes of all the world.

> *Where has your beloved gone,*
> *O fairest among women...?*

the winds seemed to sing,

> *My beloved has gone down to his garden,*
> *to the bed of spices....*

The Magdalene cupped her face in her hands, positioned for the long night's vigil.

"I must find Mary first," the thought suddenly occurred to her.

In the midst of all the recent events, the Magdalene had grown increasingly anxious about the mother of Jesus. In union with her son, she'd been fasting since the eve of Passover and hadn't slept more than an hour or two since the arrest.

Determining that her elderly charge must be persuaded out of the night's bitter chill at all costs, Miriam abandoned her perch on the ridge and lowered herself cautiously into the old quarry to look for signs of Mary and the other vigil-keepers.

A strange silence engulfed the city, as it had all afternoon since the earthquake—a silence one could feel in the bones. "Will it be any quieter at the end of the world?" she wondered.

Miriam found herself—almost against her will—drawn step by step in the direction of the place, toward the slightly raised mound outside the Genath Gate where only hours before he had hung like a carcass against the darkening sky.

Stumbling over bramble in the gloom, she nearly fell headlong over a tall, dark, wool-mantled body that lay stretched out cruciform before the Roman stipes, the permanent stake upon which the bodies of the crucified were mounted.

"Mary!" Miriam gasped, recognizing the identity of the person who lay sprawled in the darkness at the foot of the cross, arms laid out against the stones. Stillness lay over the mother of Jesus like a veil.

At first, Miriam could not even hear her breathe. The Magdalene bent down to rouse the older woman to her feet. But the terrible silence that enveloped her—the one his followers called "the Woman"—stopped her. The Magdalene retreated, unsure of what to do, conscious only of the weight of some awesome task the silence and the discovery of Mary on Golgotha had lain upon her.

In the pale light of the moon just rising over the eastern mountain, Miriam could make out the figures of other women, poised motionless on stones overlooking the site of the tomb.

Set me as a seal upon your heart,

a voice sang deep inside her,

As a seal upon your arm;
for love is strong as death.

Slowly—thought by thought, word by word—a strange conviction was growing in the Magdalene's mind. A fierce and certain knowledge it was—like that of a woman who knows in the dead of night, as her lover sleeps, that a child has been conceived. It was an almost physical sensation that vindication was being born in that darkness, that life—like a seed—was stirring in the hard black womb of the earth.

The Magdalene pulled back the heavy mantle from her brow, allowing the night breezes to play in her hair. The fallen face of Cephas—the "Rock," as the Master called him—passed across her eyes as she settled on her haunches near the body of her mistress.

"Let the Twelve huddle in their room," she said to herself. "Men are proud and impatient creatures, even the best of them. Night work is for women—the long, patient task of watching for the verdicts of heaven: birth and death, healing and sickness."

Have you seen him whom my heart loves?

she asked the silent earth, cupping her face in her hands. From her long elegant fingers came the faint scent of the perfumes with which she had anointed the Master's body after he had raised Lazarus from the dead.

⟫⟫⟫ III ⟪⟪⟪

These last words Issa heard with the ears of sleep.

For some time now, the boy's mind had been drifting in and out of slumber: the voice of the story-teller—now close, now far—as his attention wavered on the frontier of dreams.

He was still seated on cushions in the warm chapel alcove under the icon of the terebinth—of that he was sure. And though he could not see the blue-graying sky beyond the room's tiny windows, the fragrance of the air told him that the night had passed.

In the distance, the low murmur of a Moslem cantor, preparing to chant the morning call to prayer, sent the "Light Verse" aloft on the newborn sky:

> *Picture the light as a niche*
> *within which there is a lamp,*

the voice droned,

> *and the lamp is within a glass.*
> *And it is as though the glass*
> *were a glittering star*
> *lit from a sacred olive tree...*

(The voice was joined by Shukri's now)

> *"...whose oil would radiate*
> *even without the touch of fire."*

Issa smiled, leaning his head back against the old man's chest. The world was just like that, the boy thought, his head beginning to nod. A flame within a glass within a star—one light housing another....

The specter rose, dark-robed, from the shadows beneath the tree and made a ring-shaped gesture with his hands. At once, the gilded foliage of the oak disappeared and a vast wedding canopy, beaded in gold, spread itself in its place.

Was this another of Shukri's tales, Issa wondered? But the old man was nowhere to be seen. Even the chapel itself appeared to have given way to a golden hillside of crags and caves under a brilliant noon-lit sky.

Perhaps he should be afraid, then, the boy considered.

But the first thing he noticed was that the vision's right hand was raised in blessing.

Just to be sure, however, he made the sign of the cross. The specter bowed deeply and blessed him.

When he did this, Issa got a better look at him. He was wearing the simple garb of a monk, the kind one sees only in very old icons. But Issa noticed that, in place of the usual embroidered cross on his cowl, the specter wore a small Bethlehem star.

He held a long white scroll in his hand which he used to direct Issa's attention to the marble slab at the foot of the tree.

Issa felt confident enough to hazard a question.

"Are you the saint of this place," the boy heard himself stammer in a voice which did not sound at all like his. "Are you the holy Parakletos? Is this your grave...?"

The figure nodded slowly.

But at the mention of the word "grave," in no time whatever, a stiff wind arose. Issa felt its sting on his face. The monk's black mantle spread like wings before the oak.

Then he placed the huge scroll in Issa's hands.

"However am I going to open it?" Issa wondered out loud.

130

"It's too heavy."

Suddenly, the boy found, to his amazement, the great document unrolled before him. He touched its edges. The scroll felt soft as cotton. On its cloud-white surface, an inscription had been traced.

"To Issa of Nazareth," it read, "from his father...."

He awoke to the smell of coffee. Clean starched sheets and wool blankets swaddled his frame, and his head lay sunk in a vast white pillow. A quick survey of his surroundings told Issa the rest. There could be no doubt about it: he was ensconced in Shukri's old black-lacquered bed with the brass fixings. He'd admired its fantastic bulk from afar on previous visits to the house of his old friend. But he'd never dared to imagine himself buried in its sweet cotton expanses.

He reached out his hand to finger the black gloss of the acanthus-leaf pattern which curled up the iron bed post. As he did so, he noticed the blue Bethlehem star embroidered on the bed linen. It was on the pillow cases, on the borders of sheets, on everything. The sunburst star of Bethlehem, even these days the pride of that city's seamstresses, the old mark of the Christians of *terra sancta*, the emblem—so Shukri had implied—on the prayer shawl of Joseph the Just, King David's sign.

Issa settled back once more into the comfort of the pillows. What on earth could have induced the old man to put Issa to bed in his own room, the boy wondered. Always before, on the rare occasions when he'd had permission to stay with Shukri, he'd slept outside in the corridor, on the big sofa, covered with blankets and rugs.

Issa sighed with contentment. The aroma of the coffee which had awakened him stole through the white-domed room like a friendly summons. A little analysis told the boy that Shukri himself—not the cleaning lady—had prepared it. No one he knew ever ground as much fragrant cardamon into the mixture as Shukri did.

The sound of tapping in the corridor told Issa that he had a visitor. The familiar caftaned figure peered in at the boy from the open doorway. In the pale light of mid-morning, filtered through white muslin drapes, the face of Shukri looked almost youthful, the outlines of his still-sleek face highlighted against the shadows.

It was then, at that exact moment, with the merchant's face in half-light, that Issa remembered his dream, the dream of old St. Parakletos and the wedding. Shukri's countenance had brought it to mind. The bridegroom in his dream had looked like that, like Shukri looked now against the light.

"I've had a dream, Baba," Issa said to the figure in the doorway.

Shukri advanced into the room balancing a demitasse of Turkish coffee in one hand.

"Here, my son," the merchant said, smiling, feeling for the boy's face. Issa reached for the coffee and took his first sips of the dark, wide-awake brew.

It was just then that Issa detected the perfume. Shukri's habits were the soul of predictability. Perhaps that went with being blind, Issa thought. But the coffee Shukri had brought bore the unmistakable scent of rosewater. Issa's mother had been known to put a little sweetened flower-water into coffee on festive occasions. But never Shukri.

Coffee laced with scent—it was one of his earliest memories. As a small boy, he'd heard his mother say something about his father one Easter afternoon while spooning a little rosewater into a bubbling brass coffee pot. It was such a rare occurrence—she hardly ever spoke about her husband's disappearance—that her words had stayed with him all these years.

"If he must," she told a relative then, with a voice of steel, "he'll rise from the grave to find us."

But Issa was eager to tell the old man about his dream. Questions about the coffee could wait.

Shukri sat down on the edge of the bed. "A dream?" the old man said.

"Yes," cried Issa, his voice full of wonder. "I saw a wedding beneath the oak tree—you know, *our* oak. The branches had turned into a giant canopy. And the ring: I saw a slender hand place it in the heart of the tree. The monk Parakletos was there, too," he whispered. "The Fatherless. The one buried in the church."

"Your wedding dream—it had a bride and bridegroom, I trust," said Shukri in a voice so gentle it could hardly be heard.

Issa paused before he answered.

"St. Joseph and the Virgin, it seemed," the boy said hesitantly.

"Ah," the old man sighed.

"If you could only have seen it!" Issa cried. "They wore golden robes and crowns of oak leaves, and there were roses on their feet. When they moved, their clothing shone like the sun, as if it were made of mirrors."

"And their faces," Shukri persisted, "did you see their faces?"

Issa settled back into the pillows and took a deep breath.

"Yes, Baba. But when I came close to them, the faces changed. The bride had not the Virgin's face but my mother's. And the bridegroom," Issa said, turning to the merchant,"—it was you!"

Shukri said nothing at first. He just sat, his face bent towards the boy as if he were composing Issa's features in his mind.

134

"Was I still blind in your dream?" he asked, finally.

"Oh, no, Baba," Issa said, his eyes filling with tears. "Oh, no, you could see. In my dream, you could see!"

Shukri had risen from the edge of the bed. Though he hid his face from the boy, Issa could see that the old man's body shook with emotion. The merchant leaned hard on his cane trying to gain control of himself. But it was some time before his shoulders stopped heaving, before he dared to speak again.

"There once was a man from Nazareth," the merchant began, "Noel, by name. The town silversmith. I knew him well. It was known among the townspeople that Noel's ancestry could be traced back to the family of Christ—through James, the Martyr, first bishop of Jerusalem. Not that he ever referred to it himself, you understand. But...it was acknowledged."

"The family of Christ?" Issa cried.

"Yes, my child. Many members of the Nazareth branch of the family became his followers, calling themselves the Company of the Lord's Brothers. Down through the centuries, they preserved their identity in a quiet way—aware that the Master himself had forbidden them to claim special prerogatives among the believers. Nevertheless, it may be said that certain traditions of the Holy Family have been kept alive...only among them...."

Issa sat up straight in the bed. "The *ring*...."

"The ring," said Shukri, his face invisible now in a pool of shadows, "a pattern passed down the ages from the time of Joseph the Builder. On its branches they hung their own history of the Messiah's deeds."

"And the man Noel?" Issa inquired breathlessly.

Shukri paused, letting the late morning silence frame his

words. "He had many cares, beyond his years, the man who was your father."

A strong breeze—a softer version of the wind of Issa's dream—swept through the upper-story rooms like the ghost breath of the storyteller's last word.

"My father..." Issa whispered, as if beckoning a presence.

"He and your mother had been married just three days when war struck," Shukri went on evenly. "Your mother had been sent to Jerusalem to arrange a celebration there with her husband's relations. Noel was delayed in the north supervising work on their home. Suddenly, they found themselves separated.

"Against everyone's advice, Noel raced south on foot to be with his bride. Through enemy lines and mine fields, skirting patrols, he ran. In the city, they awaited him. But he never came. No one could find so much as a trace of him—a coat, a letter, a message, a grave. He had disappeared.

"Finally the war ended. Some refugees returned. Still, there was no sign of Noel.

"Everyone assumed, of course, that he had died: perhaps alone on a hillside or in a patch of woods, shot down at night while running or maimed in an olive grove.

"Perhaps he'd perished in a Syrian prison, they said, like so many of the refugees, tortured there for aiding a fellow prisoner or for trying to escape.

"Everyone assumed that he had died—everyone, that is, but your mother. To this very day, she waits for him, doesn't she?

"Well, pity is a lamp with little oil. Noel's relatives soon tired of commiserating with their widow bride. She reminded them of the dead, of the disaster, they said.

"Soon the last members of his family had left for other destinations, for safe havens from pain and want. She was left to live a refugee's life in Jerusalem, alone. It was for his sake that she stayed. Her Noel must know where to find her, she said, her husband of three days.

"A woman alone, without family, in a strange city cannot fail to inspire gossip. But when your mother's womb began to grow, then the talk grew bold and vile. She was so lovely, so gentle, so strong—it drove the envious wild.

"And then you came into the world, Issa—named, as was fitting, for your grandfather, Issa the Elder of Nazareth, called *il-Meskin*—'Poor One'—by locals for his charity, the patriarch of the family of Christ."

Even in the smoky light that morning managed to filter through the open doorway, Issa could see that Shukri's face was shining.

It had been only one day since a small boy discovered a ring embedded in the flesh of an oak, one day since a toy had become a cocoon of mysteries.

There was only one bend left to turn in the journey now, one last question to be asked.

Issa sat on the edge of the bed, facing his friend.

"Baba," he said, "how do you know these things?"

The question hung in the air.

"Tell me, please," Issa cried, on his feet.

"I once knew a proud and foolish merchant," said Shukri. (The words were uttered one by one, with great effort.) "He had been blinded in his youth and his body bore other, more hidden, marks of war. Children shouted after him:

Old man, blind man,

"Young men—yet not much younger than himself—had to guide him about like a grandfather.

"But the tradesman's war-scarred hands soon learned again the jeweler's skill passed down to him by his forebears. And the eyesight of his heart full of wounds proved superior to that which had been taken in the olive grove.

"He began to be well-off, this young man, old before his time.

"Then one day he heard a voice in the street, a woman's voice, a simple thing, the call of a mother to her distant child. 'Issa..., Issa....'

"The blind merchant nearly went out of his mind. He came crashing out of his shop without his cane, upsetting barrels of merchandise, scattering coins in every direction as he hurled himself after that voice. He was known as a dignified, sober person. No one had ever seen him behave this way before. People began to run after him, afraid that he would stumble on the paving stones, afraid that he would fall. 'Stop! Stop!' they cried. There was such a tumult around him, in fact, that the poor man lost track completely of the thin ribbon of sound which had summoned him from his shop. He fell, despairing, in the middle of the street.

"Strange, yes?

"But you see, Issa, the merchant had heard the voice of his wife in the cacophony of the street that day—the wife he had lost in the war. He recognized her instantly, from the sound of a single syllable on her lips. The memory of that voice, that sound, had been his sustenance through years of imprisonment and torture and exile.

"Shopkeepers helped him to his feet. (His head was bleeding badly.) Someone began to daub his face with a handkerchief. There was a voice close by, at his ear: 'Have you hurt yourself, father?' (He was trembling.) It was she!

"He wanted to embrace her, to shout, to reveal himself then and there in front of everyone. But—as I told you—he was proud and foolish, Issa. His blindness and his wounds prevented him.

"'She was the bride of three days,' he reminded himself. 'The man she once knew, the youth she wed, was swift and strong. In return for her devotion, shall I offer her now the gift of a sightless old man?'"

These last words faded into silence. The pressure of feeling had robbed the merchant of his voice.

As for Issa, he too was speechless. Every object, every sound, the baubles of light which flickered on the walls—all seethed with a strange vitality. Thought was impossible.

Over and over again, Issa tried to say the word "father" to the man before him. "Baba," papa—it should have been so easy to say the word. But all the boy had inside him now were feelings, not words. And they would not speak.

But what was clear to him, even now, was that for the first time in his life he was not afraid.

Noel took his son's hand as Issa led him down the long stone stairs to the courtyard open to the sky. It was noon, time for the midday meal. The clear, blue-tinted air was permeated with the scent of garlic and mint and roasting meat.

Issa drew water from the courtyard well for his father's ablutions. They washed together, father and son.

From the open doorway that led to the dining room, Issa heard a familiar snatch of melody borne on an even more familiar voice:

Now,
now the shroud is flying;
the cloths that bound him
dance,
dance,
O canopy of butterflies....

It was an Easter song, one of the songs the women sing on Easter Monday when they clean their homes with scented water. The identity of the singer was no mystery. It was Myrna's voice, the voice of Issa's mother coming from beyond the doorway.

She was busy setting the table for lunch, her arms laden with dishes of cool minted cucumber and fresh tomatoes and the bitter Jerusalem olive, with platters of grilled fish and plates piled high with bread. In the center of the table was a blue ceramic bowl filled with fresh cut lemons. And everywhere, there were flowers.

She'd not yet detected their presence in the courtyard.

Noel signaled for his son to be very, very quiet. He was savoring the sound of his bride's voice as if her song itself were a feast. For some minutes, the two stood in the open doorway as the woman arranged the merchant's fine porcelain on the white linen tablecloth.

Issa could tell from her manner that she had been told everything. All her movements seemed unsteady, newborn, stunned with happiness.

"Tell him everything," her note to the merchant had read. Issa smiled to think that "everything" had proved more, much more, than even his mother had dreamed. But perhaps—and this was the first time the idea had stepped fully out of the shadows of his thoughts—she'd known all along. More even than Noel.

Just then she lifted her hand to sweep back a strand of hair from her forchead. As she did so, Issa spotted the ring, *his ring*—he'd almost forgotten it—the ring he had found one noon in the shade of the terebinth tree, rising now on his mother's hand like a flame.

AUTHOR'S NOTE

Should an inquisitive reader wish to discover the inspiration behind these stories, he or she has but to search out the famous Terebinth altarpiece of the Nazarene artist Issa en-Nasri in a small subterranean Orthodox chapel off Christian Quarter Road, Jerusalem. The more adventuresome reader may even wish to seek the great terebinth itself along the bridal path between Nazareth and Tiberias.

The author cannot, of course, provide precise directions to either destination.